Jigsaw Men

A Novella

John Tessitore

This is a slightly edited version of the first edition, begun in 2007, published quietly in 2012, and just as quietly withdrawn from public view. I revisit it now because elements of the story echo recent events, including the Covid-19 pandemic and the accelerating deterioration of the environment. I find the coincidences interesting and hope you will too.

I.

I'd seen it all before—the sunlight pouring through empty houses, strip malls collapsing, bridges rusting and coming apart—but it never failed to shock me: the squalor that followed defeat. Half way to Glenden, the suburbs were like a photographic negative, tattered and lush in all the wrong places. Road signs were down or swallowed by the coarse, opportunistic vines that now had the run of the place. Long shadows darkened landmarks, hid intersections. Major arteries were clogged by debris, some were completely impassable, some had simply vanished.

Map routes were useless and GPS was hacked so often it was a mere vagary now, an idea whose time had come and gone, like vaccinations or world peace.   I was left to my instincts, feeble as they were. In all the time I spent negotiating the twists and turns to Glenden, I didn't see a soul, not a single person who could have given me directions, suggested a shortcut, or told me to forget it all and git while the gittin' was still good.

I'd left my apartment knowing there was no margin for error. For the day or days to come, I was to be on a budget even more limited than usual and the waste of a few wrong turns was potentially devastating, a fortune in fuel. And yet I erred anyway, drove in circles for the better part of an hour, and was in a foul mood when I finally found Nate's house.

It was a stately place sitting forward on a rocky elevation high above the road. Behind it loomed a dark wood and a sky flaking like an orange rind, opaque and blushing, with a little drop of poison. On the ground, there were hints of a late-May renewal. Buds were just beginning to open. Yellow pollen was gathering in the crooks of exposed rocks and a green tint shaded black branches. But everything was still except for that roiling sky, feathered like the face of Jupiter, and me in my lunar buggy. I eased the car around a bend at the top of the driveway, drove over a sink of asphalt shards and rubble, and parked beneath a bare, gray tree.

It was a two-ply afternoon for sure. Although I'd been wearing a mask on and off for a year or more back home—in the city, where things had never been quite habitable—there was something particularly disheartening about the requirement here in a place like Glenden, the point of which had always been health and hygiene, thick hair and a rosy complexion. To wear a mask here was to turn one's back on a dream. Stubbornly, I left mine in the glove compartment and hurried up Nate's front steps. As I pressed the doorbell, I could feel my throat catch as if I'd swallowed a pushpin.

Waiting with my back to the door, I could see the land pucker and fold in three directions: to the west, woods and stone fences boxing the hillsides; to the east, shingled roofs and a white steeple in the distance; and just across the road, through a stand of waking trees, a small farm: a greenhouse and a couple of tool sheds rotting in the haze, a few acres of yellowy stalks and straw, the husks of last years crops still lying fallow on the ground. All of it foreign to me, the way the past is foreign, but welcome too, a sight for sore city eyes. Very sore all of a sudden.

No one came to the door so I knocked again, louder this time, and listened for the sounds of motion inside. What I heard instead came from somewhere behind me, a sinister grind lifting out of the silence. Headlights were oozing through the branches a quarter mile off, creeping around a bend and coming straight for me. A police car, black and white. I panicked as if I had something to hide.

It stopped on the shoulder of the road opposite Nate's house and a young man, a scarecrow wearing a holster, slid out from behind the wheel and headed into the fields. I watched him as he walked the perimeter and then along the crop rows. He was wearing a paper surgeon's mask and, despite the fading light, sunglasses, and was using a flashlight to search the deeper shadows. From where I was standing, I could have told him he was wasting his time. There were no thieves lurking in the darkness that evening; there were no crops to steal.

The door clicked behind me. A pair of dimly lit eyes studied me from a narrow opening. "You're here?" he croaked, pulling the door wider. He was wearing an ancient cardigan, maroon and pilled, against a crisp white shirt and khaki pants ironed to a razor crease. His hair, salt-and-pepper, was combed flat and rigid with teeth marks. Freshly shaven, he had missed a spot behind his jawbone where a little hillock of whisker lent some character to the otherwise bland, pleasing contours of his face. He stood bolt upright, his shoulders back, almost sprightly in his attention except that he was staring at my shoulder. And he kept staring as he heaved and hacked into a yellow handkerchief he pulled from his pants pocket.

"Pardon me," he said after clearing his throat. "I'm susceptible on nights like this. Just not myself. But it is nice to finally meet you."

He had a very firm handshake and he twisted my arm a bit as he held me, as if he were trying to read more than my palm alone would allow.

"How are you faring?" he asked.

"Not too badly. Only a tickle in my throat."

"Well, please come inside before it gets worse. By all means. Yes."

He shuffled backwards into the vestibule on silk socks, also maroon, but riddled with holes. I shuffled in behind him.

"I'm quite lucky," he said. "These windows aren't new. Not by a long shot. We must have replaced them over fifteen years ago. Nevertheless, they manage to keep out the worst of it. I find I'm able to breathe quite normally most of the time, and when I can't I just take a nap."

The close, warm vestibule gave way to a long hall branching into a series of small, preciously decorated rooms, each a kind of museum display. Wainscoting and crown molding, sideboards and mantles, chairs with ball-and-claw feet, framed paintings of red barns and by-passed gas stations, parquet flooring—everything dovetailed or pegged or morticed or tenoned or carved or beveled or polished or distressed had a home here, where all was heavy and hardwood.

"This is a beautiful place," I said.

"Oh come now," he answered over his shoulder as he led me to the kitchen. "It's Colonial Williamsburg. A replica of an idea of a history. Ridiculous. Almost a good thing I can't see it anymore."

There was a table by the front door, a place to drop car keys and gloves, and separate baskets for incoming and outgoing mail. The baskets were empty but beneath the table was a small pile of fallen fliers and leaflets. On top of the pile, the uncanny: "Edifice Wrecks Demolition. A mom-and-pop production. 'Let's tear it down together.' 555-6354."

"We did this when we were flush," Nate was saying. "You should see the bedroom upstairs. All the dark portraits of stern Presbyterians, purchased at an antique fair in the hills thirty years ago or more. A forbidding bunch, especially when you wake up in the middle of the night and their eyes are following you to the loo. They made me feel like one of Hawthorne's heroines, like I could lose my virtue at any moment, even under the ancestors' watchful eyes. But Walter loved them, said they reminded him of his parents. He was being ironic, of course. Everything we did once upon a time was ironic. In fact, Walter's parents were wonderful people. And Catholics to boot. But we're never quite satisfied with our parents, are we."

A tarnished tea kettle was whistling as we entered a kitchen strangled in wicker and dried herb, baskets hanging from exposed beams, sprays of brittle flowers tucked into every crevice. Nate hacked again, turned off the stovetop. As the whistle faded, I heard the music for the first time. It was coming from somewhere down the hall.

"We always turn our parents into stern Presbyterians. You'll have a cup of tea?"

The sound was a century old at least, a fluttering, swaggering clarinet and then a muffled trumpet. The room, so heavy with old things, one toile curtain away from absolute kitsch, seemed lighter suddenly, as if it were about to take flight. "I know this," I said.

"I should hope you do. It's Gershwin."

"Something Rhapsody."

"In Blue."

"It was a commercial for plane tickets when I was a kid."

"Of course it was. Where else have you heard it? Bugs Bunny?"

"Maybe."

"Oh my. If you ask me, this is exactly why all the important music went east, along with money and war. Because of things like plane tickets and television commercials. I don't even like Gershwin, myself, but he deserves our respect. Bugs Bunny too, come to think of it. The giants of our culture."

He filled two porcelain cups with boiling water. "I only have Earl Gray," he said, dropping a bag into a cup and handing the cup to me. "You can't find a decent avocado anymore, or a sweet bunch of grapes, and a good, tart lemon is worth its weight in ivory. But you can still get Earl Gray by the case. I credit the British. They've always had their priorities in order. Sugar's on the counter. Take all you want. I never use it."

He led me to a parlor behind the kitchen, where we sat in wing-backed chairs before a cold, stone hearth. Gershwin was playing somewhere in that room, though I couldn't find the source. "I can't live without my music," he said as the piano pranced, then tinkled to a slow blues. "It's all I have now that Walter's gone. Walter and my vision, both gone around the same time. But I had my music then, and I still do. These days, it seems I only want to hear the

Americans, Copland, a few of the later composers, Adams when he's serious, and Ives of course. Always Ives. The artist as insurance agent. I can identify with that. Yes. Ives, Copland, Adams. Gershwin. That's the program for the season." He took a sip from his cup and smiled at the floor. "You haven't the slightest idea what I'm talking about, do you?"

"No. Not really."

"Maybe I'll teach you."

"I don't know how long I'll be around."

"Longer than you think, I'm sure," Nate said. We sat listening to the piano like a jet among the clouds. "Lovely," he said, his red-rimmed eyes going rheumy. "Obvious, but in a lovely way." Then, abruptly, he turned his face to mine. "I'm sorry I woke you up last night. I wasn't in a good frame of mind, and you were the only person I thought to call. I've pulled myself together since then and shipped your father off to the crematorium, so you don't have to worry about that. But now that you're here, you still have a job to do. And you should plan to stay as long as it takes to get the job done. It's time for all of us to make our peace."

He'd sounded younger on the phone. Everyone sounded raspy these days, but on the phone Nate's rasp had a little of the piccolo in it, to use a metaphor he'd have appreciated, a little of the wood sprite. There was none of that now—courtly manners and a dreamy bookishness, but nothing that resembled vitality, let alone youth.

"What did he do for you?" I asked.

"Yes," he said. "To business. Plenty of time to get acquainted later." He cleared his throat, this time without convulsion. "Where to begin? Well, take a look at me Mr. Stark. How much do you think I can do for myself?" Stiffly, he crossed his legs and shifted in his seat. His teacup sloshed in his hand but he didn't spill a drop. "You see, I realized before most people that our circumstances had changed. Irrevocably. Because of the blindness, I needed a helping hand before most people did, and that gave me a new perspective, figuratively speaking of course. And that's where George came in."

He craned his neck around the wing of the chair and set his eyes on my throat. Fortunately, he couldn't see me squirm.

"You never met him?" he asked.

"I don't remember him at all," I replied.

"So this won't be too disturbing for you to hear? Because George had many good qualities, and also many bad ones. His kindness to me, as it developed over time, was a good quality. The drinking was a bad one. Essentially, he was lazy. That was the root of everything else that had ever happened to him, or that hadn't happened to him. So he was a flawed man, but I believe he was a good man on balance. Do you still want me to continue?"

"Please do. I have no personal stake in this story. I can take it."

"It is my hope that you will come to have a personal stake in this story," Nate said then, sharply, like a schoolteacher.

I stood up and paced the room, sweaty with the realization that I was being manipulated, perhaps as my father had been manipulated. Nate listened for a moment as I circled his chair, the floorboards giggling beneath my feet. Then he continued. "I met George at the edge of the woods one morning. He was sleeping at the foot of a tree, but snoring so loudly that I was able to avoid tripping over him as I hobbled by. Let's be honest about this now. He was sleeping off a bender, and who knows how much alcohol he'd poured down his gullet. My first thought was that there was a wounded deer before me, such was the sound he was making. But no creature of the forest has ever smelled like that man did, and that's when I became truly afraid. What does an old blind man do to protect himself from a rancid, drunken derelict? I hit him with my walking stick." He chuckled at the memory. "Can you believe it? I hit the sleeping man three times, I know not where on his poor body, before he woke up screaming bloody murder. But he didn't hit me back, which was kind of him, so I apologized and invited him inside for a cup of tea and some soap. Understand something now. All that has happened to us in this new epoch of ours has happened exceptionally quickly. So you can imagine my surprise, my shock to find a homeless man roaming my woods. Today they're as common, more common than houseflies. Marauders all. But just a few years ago, they were problems one came to places like Glenden to escape. Yet I did not ask him where he'd been, what he'd done, whom he'd wronged. I only asked him where he was going. Since he had no answer, I offered him the cabin out back, the guest quarters Walter had built for his sister when she was recovering from her stroke. As I said, he could have dealt with me rather easily when I caned him, but he restrained himself so I knew he was trustworthy. I told him he could live there as long as he helped a queer old blind man survive in a broken world."

"And he stayed," I said, sitting again and smiling in spite of myself.

"He assaulted me with the most vicious language I'd heard in a long while, something about manhood and freedom and the American Way and other such nonsense, sprinkled generously with four letter words, some of which were brand new to me. But, yes, he stayed. He and his many problems settled into the cabin out back, where he stayed for the next five years, until his problems killed him."

"There!" he gasped suddenly, pointing to a tune now charging through the air. "That's not Gerswhin anymore. That's Adams now. Adams being coy and cagey."

He listened in rapture while I went back over what he'd just told me, a story sifted through a crescendo of trumpets and snare drums and tweeting flutes.

"How did you find me?" I asked.

"George always knew where you were. Somehow, he kept track."

"Did he leave much behind? Lots of stuff to sort through?"

Nate grinned and turned away from me, toward the empty fireplace. "Just you wait," he said. "As I told you, you'll be here longer than you think."

II.

May 27, ----

We have previously written to you regarding the debt referred to below, however, you have chosen not to respond. Your lack of attention to this matter has left us no alternative but to assume that this debt is valid and legally owed to your creditor. If any reason exists for not paying this balance IN FULL, it is your responsibility to contact this office immediately, otherwise we strongly suggest you PAY THIS BALANCE IMMEDIATELY!!

NLA Financial Systems Inc/Southward Emergency Physicians
$395.00

June 8, ----

*We are writing to remind you that payment has not been received
for your current utility bill. This bill is now past due and should
be paid immediately to avoid possible interruption of your service
and additional charges. The amount past due is shown in the
box of the lower right-hand portion of this letter.*

Tolkin Electric Cooperative Inc.
$34.35

3/2/--
Brother,

I finally got over the first shock of receiving your letter of nine months. But no kidding it was good to hear from you. If you think your bad about writing I'm terrible. Also cain't spell shit. Also.

Thanks a lot for letting me get some kind of word from you.

Brother—believe me, I was getting worried, and maybe still am. I sure wish things were better for you:: Hell I wish things were better for me also. But what the hell, compared to what I used to be, I'm not doing to bad I guess. At least now I'm working and trying to save a little money for a rainy day.

Also glad to hear your kids are O.K. As we both know already, kids always ajust its their mothers & fathers that have a terrible time with fucking their lives up, and really that is what anyone does when they go through a divorce. Fuck their lives up.

My marriage was so long ago it seems like another life time. Were three for three, brother. Some pair, ain't we?

Billy is still working for Edison and is doing very well for himself. He's also making some good decisions for himself.

My little Jenny is at State "junior" year and is <u>enjoying</u> it thank <u>God</u>. I might get one through college.

Barb works for a doctor in Fort William. She does the filing. She seems to be doing a little better than she was. Maybe one day things will be better.

Jimmy & his family is the most screwed up family north of 92 and theirs no hope in sight. We all know that and so does he.

Well Brother theres nothing but gossip & shit I can write about for you so will close.

If you can some weekend maybe we can see one another at the camp, or come down here. This place isn't so bad you just have to over look a few things.

Work 7 days a week makes a long month, but what else do I have to do. I can get all the pussy I want & need in 3 or 4 minutes & that takes care for another month or so. When you reach my age we just think & talk about it.

Everyone in Colby is well—except getting older—colds, etc.

Thanks again for the letter and really Brother don't go this long again without keeping in touch.

Tell the kids hi & Uncle Billy loves them. Maybe one of these days I can get by to see them again.

Brother take care & write, call, or come see me—

Billy

These were the first three pieces of paper I picked up off the floor, each of them in their original envelopes and dated around the same time, almost four decades earlier, the first a couple of years after I was born. They were yellowing around the edges with slight tears in the folds, and the letter from Billy was streaked with a rust color that could have been blood, or it could have been rust. But all were legible. The envelopes, on the other hand, had born the full brunt of my father's life and were smeared with gold and brown and even grass stains, as if they'd been dragged great distances over mountains and prairies to be dumped on the floor of this small cabin in the clearing behind Nate's house.

Nate had offered to put me up in the main house where, he said, I'd be "less likely to putrefy." But I told him I'd feel more comfortable knowing that I wasn't intruding on his privacy, and that maybe I'd get to know my father better if I lived in his rooms for a while. That's what I thought he'd want to hear, insistent as he was that I take a personal interest in my own past. Instead, he chuckled with what I thought was undue hostility and led me back to the cabin so that I could see my father's natural habitat for myself.

We followed a stone walkway across a calico of shadow, through untended gardens overrun with tall grasses shining blond in the moonlight. The cabin stood a hundred feet from Nate's back door, behind and to the west of the house. It was a small, shed-like structure, vinyl sided and tightly joined, neat if not exactly clean. On its face hung a faded wooden plaque of a fat hausfrau holding a sign that read "Willkommen." Nate jiggled a key in the lock. "Nice night," he said. "It's sad to me that we never fail to notice a nice night anymore." When he pushed the door open, we both fell back in retreat from the stench.

I kept my distance as Nate reached into the darkness. He ran his hand along the wall inside the doorway, then flipped a light switch to reveal the great wreckage, a heaping pile of trash where a room should have been. It was geologic in its mass and also in the story it had to tell, preserving the years—most wasted, clearly—in sedimentary layers of refuse: lottery scratch-offs, unopened Christmas cards, hunting bullets, junk mail, clothing, rifle parts, baseball caps, nibbled pencils, scraps of paper (phone numbers, lists of names, algebraic equations), a vacuum-sealed package of green bologna, expired cans of precooked pasta, spit cups caked with tobacco sludge, a bong, tattered books, baby pictures. And bottles. Dozens and dozens of plastic bottles, all empty. Bottles holding the piles together like bricks in a mortar of filth. It was a grand monument to a ruined life and in its own way a real achievement.

"What the hell?" I said.

"Obviously I've never seen it. But I can smell it, and I've tapped around it a bit. Is it as profound as I imagine it to be?"

"It's a tomb," I said.

"Ah, but an Egyptian one. Your father spent the last five years collecting things to take with him into the next life."

"This is more than five years' worth of stuff."

"Yes. He had some in storage somewhere. A friend's basement, I think. It was all crammed into plastic bags for the move, according to some system he could never remember. It's a funny thing. About garbage, he actually had some ambition." He paused, but I said nothing. "You blame me, but this was part of our deal. He took care of me, and I left him alone."

"I don't blame you. I already know you better than I ever knew him."

"I bet you'll know him pretty well after you sort through this."

"Not sure I want to know him now."

"I don't believe that," Nate said. "I think George was more interesting for his flaws."

He could hear me rustling around in all the paper, kicking the pile with my work boot. "Are you certain you want to stay here?" he asked.

"No," I said, "but I'll stay here anyway."

"Then I shall retire, and leave you to get acquainted with a complicated man."

"Do you need help getting back?"

"This is my home, sir. I know the way."

I stood in the center of the cabin for a long time after Nate left, surveying the battlefield of a slow, suicidal conflict. Tin foil like twisted steel. Cellophane like barbed wire. For half a decade, my father had stood where I was standing, pouncing and battering himself until he was nothing but the debris I'd been called in to sort and clear. I doubted that I'd ever be able to put him back together, not in any way he'd have recognized.

I cleaned off a recliner, pushed some papers, plastic wrappers, and a moldy bath towel to the floor, and sat down to read the three scraps I picked up first. I stared at them for a while, turned them over in my hands, took a deep breath and sniffed them before I opened them. I read them each three times in search of a thread, something I could tug and trace through the weave: in the space of one year, my father had been injured but couldn't, or wouldn't, pay for the care he'd received; had a home but couldn't, or wouldn't, pay for utilities; and received a letter from an older brother who appears to have been as conscientious as he was, who was nine months late in responding to an eagerly-awaited letter from my father (also late), but who had some reason to be just as worried as ever about my father's well-being, even after receiving my father's letter. Three pieces of mail, but even the scant evidence before me confirmed my mother's most bitter accusations, leveled against the entire Stark clan in the wee hours of the morning when I'd find her sleepless at the kitchen table, a glittery paperback unread on the table before her. "My poor Will," she'd say. "You come from damaged stock."

Other things in that room caught my eye: a beaded satchel, a cheap souvenir from some Native American gift shop; a black mug printed with the words "Coldwater

Canyon" and crusted with coffee sediment; a single dart with a reflective skull and crossbones on its flight. Taped to a wall by the door was a piece of lined white paper, a hand-drawn grid x'd and o'd like an elaborate game of tic-tac-toe. Beneath it was a large plastic bucket containing four or five hand trowels and a green military spade. Resting on the couch was a brand new, bright yellow chain saw, never fueled. But I kept returning to the three papers I held in my hand, and particularly to the letter, a two-sided affair and something more too. I kept looking for another page, so strong was my sense that I was holding more than met the eye. And then I saw it, and realized that what was most troubling was exactly what the eye met: "kids." I hadn't recognized the word the first dozen times I'd read it, hadn't registered its meaning. George was a stranger to me, as was Billy, so I'd been reading like a voyeur, someone who wasn't personally involved in the exchange. But I *was* involved, and intimately, and was even referenced a few times. Me, and someone else. "Kids." Plural. Me, and someone else.

How is the only child of divorced parents supposed to feel about that? Nauseated, as it turned out. Sweaty and cold and unable to focus. And nauseated most of all.

I lost track of time. If my father hadn't drained every drop of alcohol from the plastic bottles he left behind I'd have poured myself a drink or three. Sober, I was staring at the ceiling—which George had not ignored, covered as it was with food stains, another vast canvas for his anti-art—wondering what to do next when the siren sounded. Ten o'clock. The blackout hour. The return of the dark ages along the eastern seaboard. Dutifully, I bolted the door and switched off the light. Only now does it occur to me that I could have lit a candle, if I'd known where to find one. But in a firetrap full of castoffs and throwbacks, I never came across even the smallest stub of wax. And so, like my father before me, I allowed myself to fall asleep in a broken recliner, surrounded by trash, come what may.

III.

I woke to the sounds of laughing, squealing children.

White light framed the window shades but when I drew them up to see what was on the other side, the old windows were cloudy with dirt, age, and the ravages of our peculiar precipitation. The glare was hot and completely opaque. Though my apartment in the city was little more than a closet and a few pipes, I'd never felt so claustrophobic at home as I did in that moment, waking in a cabin like a space station, cut off from the vastness of the universe. I began to prowl in a cold panic, checking every window and finding the same hermetic conditions everywhere—no view, no draft, no sound except for the faint, muffled shrieking of kids at play. The only way for anything to get in or out was the front door, which I now threw open, forgetting the dangers, to a day as searing as any in recent memory.

The laughter was coming from the farm across the street, where there was such a great bustle of activity that I choked back a joyful noise. About two-dozen women were wandering the crop rows, many with little children in tow, stooping to work the soil around some new-grown plants. They were talking—I could hear them now as well—but quietly, as if a word misspoken would crush the whole enterprise to dust. The children had no such compunction, however; they were running roughshod, exactly the way they were supposed to, and no one was stopping them.

I rubbed the sleep from my eyes and, for a minute or two, watched from behind the half-opened door. After some confused deliberation, I descended the broken path to the street and crossed to the fields. A few children ran past me, then turned and watched me go by, their mouths agape. I tried to smile at them but something went awry. They ran away howling.

The mothers too were wary and watching me even when they appeared to be looking away. They kept talking as if they took no notice, but I could feel their eyes.

I stepped over three beds of freshly-hoed dust and walked up to an elderly woman in a broad straw hat who was clearly the head of the operation. A field marshal in denim and calico, she was holding forth on a new pest infestation, a great swarm of "buggies," to a group of women who were hanging on her every word. When she saw me coming she shielded her round face from the light and eyed me with a mischievous twinkle. I suddenly realized I didn't know what to say.

"Can I help you?" she asked. I must have had a wild, happy gleam in my eyes. Something about me made her want to laugh.

"I'm just looking around," I said. "I'm staying with Nate for a few days, the blind guy up the hill."

"I know Nate."

"I noticed everyone working and came to see what was going on."

She knitted her brow and smiled suspiciously.

"I thought maybe you needed a hand," I said, wondering, even as I said it, why her approval was suddenly so important to me, why the first thing I'd do upon meeting her was volunteer my services—and dubious, carpenter's apprentice services at that.

"How do you know Nate?"

I hesitated, but didn't see a way around the truth. No plausible lie came to mind, and this spry old woman looked as if she would strike at the first lie to cross her path. "My father used to live in the cabin out back."

Her eyes widened and her mouth dropped to a little o. "You're George's son?"

"I am, but I don't know if that's considered a good thing or a bad thing around here. I didn't really know him."

"Well I did," she said. "And he was an asshole. Honest to God." Then she smiled again. "But I never knew a more honest asshole in my life. In fact, he helped me plan this place after the rationing started, helped me transform it and make it what it used to be. I trusted him with the well-being of every person in this quarter, and I miss him. As long as he didn't have to do any actual work, he was aces. I'm Betsy."

She took off her work gloves and shook my hand. I felt like I was holding the bark of a very old tree. "Will," I said.

"Good to meet you, Will. George's son. A son of George who actually wants to do something. This really is the end of the world."

"Well, as I said, I didn't know him."

"It's a sad thing anyway, losing a parent."

"I've done it before."

"Doesn't make it any easier. So what is it? Trying to work off some of your sadness?"

"I don't know about that."

"You know the difference between a carrot and a weed?"

"I hope so."

"Good enough. If you really want to help, follow me."

She led me to a line of small, green plumes about thirty yards into the field. "You get one shot with carrots, Will. Can't replant 'em once they're out of the ground. So if you pull the wrong thing, you're depriving someone in this quarter of some much-needed vitamin A. Got it?"

"Got it."

"Good. Now drop to your hands and knees and get to work. And give me a holler if you have any questions."

She looked me over again and I knew I was on trial. I wasn't sure I was up to the job, or even what the job was. My mouth was sour, my back was still aching from a long night spent on a lumpy lounger, my brain was just beginning to grind into gear, and somehow I found myself nose-to-nose with six or seven lady bugs, some red with black spots, some yellow, all basking in the warmth of an unexpected morning glory. They were perched on a broad, leafy stalk that could not have been a carrot plant, and they seemed so content in their stillness that I scrupled to uproot their roost. I looked around for reassurance, but Betsy was gone; I could hear her chattering a few rows away, marveling at the resilience of her strawberry plants.

I must have looked forlorn, or ill, because someone asked if I was okay.

She had thick red hair so dark it was almost brown, and hazel eyes, and a clear, soothing, purring voice made for radio. Like everyone else except me, she was wearing a straw hat, but hers was thrown back on her head so that the brim shaded the back of her neck and her perilously bare, freckled shoulders. Sweat sparkled across the bridge of her nose. Having worked her way down the row in now time, she was only a few plants away from me.

"Huh?" I said.

"Are you okay?"

"Yeah. I'm fine. I'm just trying to figure out how the hell I got here."

"Betsy roped you in?"

"I guess so. I'm staying across the street for a few days and came to see what was happening down here. Next thing I know, I'm passing judgment on carrots and their killers, and I'm about to disturb the sleep of some innocent ladybugs."

"Don't worry about them."

"Who?"

"The ladybugs. Just pull the weeds. Pretty doesn't count for anything anymore." I looked at her again but she didn't notice. "If you can't eat it, beat it. That's what we always say. Make room for food."

"You're right. I know. It's just that I'm from the city, and this is an adjustment."

"It's an adjustment either way," she said. Her skin was so white it blazed. Everyone was pale, deliberately so, but her skin, minus the freckles, was the color of the snow that never fell anymore. "We're constantly adjusting to new conditions out here."

"I guess that's right. But this is better than the city," I said, finally getting up the nerve to tug at the offending plant and scatter the bugs to the quiet that surrounded us. "At least you know what you're dealing with. No great conspiracies. Either the stuff is growing or it's not."

She stopped working and stared at me. I took this as evidence of agreement, mistakenly, and continued. "In the city, the whole crisis can seem like a bad case of urban blight. Empty shelves and violent crime. It's all so misleading. You forget what's really happening out here."

"I don't know if that's better or worse," she said. "I have two kids. Sometimes I think it'd be a lot better for us if we didn't know what we know. Just live out the rest of our days in ignorance or complacency, at least something closer to comfort. Even a temporary comfort would suit me fine."

"Easier. But not better." I was getting the hang of it now and working more quickly, separating weed from crop and leaving a thin, low line of yellow-green crinoline in my wake. A ruffle of carrot tops on the blowaway soil. "It's better to be honest and face the future with dignity."

"Do you really believe any of that?"

"Not really. It's better when dignity's not even an issue. But I do respect your efforts."

She sat up on her heels, a sturdy woman about my age, and pulled her hair away from her face. A small mole on her cheek, just above her jawline, reminded me of someone I once knew. "The right thing for me to do is to do what I can. That's what I keep telling myself. And as long as my kids are reasonably healthy, I'm gonna keep doing what I can. Whatever I can. If that means I have to work this field, I'll do it. But this is a losing proposition and we all know it, and I'll be the first in-line at the Stop & Shop the moment one of my kids gets the belly-ache."

She was beautiful in that light and I offered a sad smile to match her own. I don't know why we were talking that way. People adrift in the same sinking boat don't usually discuss all the leaks—at least not at first. But she and I had already said a few things that most people had, by then, stopped saying. And it seemed to me that she wanted to say even more, like she'd been waiting for me.

I held out my hand and was about to introduce myself when we were distracted by the sound of an approaching car. Another black and white. It rolled to a halt beneath a withered oak and another scarecrow got out: cowboy hat, sunglasses, synthetic uniform clinging to his bones. He was followed by a tall man with the long face of a penitent, equine but baggy, with a wattle-in-progress. Horseface was wearing a baseball cap with an official patch over the bill, mirrored sunglasses with metal frames, a wrinkled white shirt, cheap trousers. The bureaucracy had arrived.

"Oh shit," she said. "This is what gets to me. This is the thing I can't get past."

Everyone was standing now, two dozen women exchanging angry glances, and even the kids held still as Betsy strode across the field for a confrontation. She was a squat little woman but she held her head high and pushed her hat down on her head. As she walked, she removed her gloves with elegant deliberation and said, in a voice loud enough for everyone to hear, "Gentlemen, how can I help you?"

Horseface looked sheepish and took off his sunglasses as Betsy approached him. He was older than he appeared before I could see his eyes, which were shrunken with time and watered in the glare. "Sorry to interrupt your work, ma'am. But I need to check your production numbers again."

"You checked them last week."

"That's what makes it a weekly check, ma'am. We've been over this."

"It's planting season, for God's sake. What could have changed in a week?"

"That's not the point, ma'am."

"Stop ma'am-ing me, David."

"That's not the point, Betsy. And you know it's not. They want me to check your papers once a week."

"To make sure this place is still floundering without their interference."

"I don't know anything about that."

"Oh, gimme a break. Come on, David. Follow me."

As they walked to a shed by the side of the road—Betsy and her armed escort—the red head turned to me and said, "Isn't this the worst part?"

"It is," I said, even though it was the most familiar thing I'd seen all morning. What could be more natural than a little red tape and a functionary full of self-importance? I'd been manhandled by too many of his brethren to feel anything but amused now. The thugs were pushing seventy here in the hinterland. The nice people of Glenden were losing their innocence to the aged, the shriveled and the disheveled. Back home, we'd have lit his clothes on fire and kicked him as he rolled.

"Hey," she said then. "You don't have any block on." She pointed to a red line forming around my bicep.

"I wasn't thinking about doing any farming when I walked over here."

"Well go get some before you fry," she said. "I'll tell Betsy you'll be back?"

"Yeah."

"Go. Go now."

IV.

"Ah, yes," Nate was saying as he spooned some oatmeal into a bowl. "The feisty Miss Elizabeth." He pushed the bowl across the counter. "It was hotter before and I'd heat it up again but there have been power surges all morning. Anyway, it's all I have until the delivery comes at noon. You may as well finish it up. At least it will stick to your ribs. So you met my dear Betsy. It is one of the remaining comforts, knowing that the world has finally come to rest on the shoulders of people like her."

From the parlor came the call of an unmuted horn, slow and plaintive, and falling strings.

"I've known Betsy for thirty years. She was a particular favorite of Walter's, who had a real appreciation for good heads and sharp tongues, and she has both. In Walter's campy days, it was all Lauren Bacall. You've heard of her, I hope. Betty Joan Perske. A tough lady in slim-fit slacks. We owned her entire career on DVD. Later, and for similar reasons, he settled into a fascination with Betsy. But he and I were the only ones. Everyone else thought she was a real bitch. Or worse, a lesbian. There she was every morning, tending her land while he and I were sitting in the front window, drinking our coffee and reading our newspapers, watching her from behind the movie reviews. She wasn't entirely unattractive in the early days, but she transformed herself into a beast of burden. To all the other people in this town she was puttering in a garden of prime acreage, land ripe for development, and frittering away a potential windfall in tax revenue. Walter and I appreciated that she was saving our panoramic views. She must have rejected a thousand offers for those acres. She fought off the vultures at town meetings for years, and tried to get them to change their ways. Saint of the rivers. Martyr of the fields. And then, one day, all at once or so it seemed, everyone actually started listening to her. It was too late, of course. The air was already full of heavy metals and the river was glowing in the dark. But they came running to her then, and they sat at her feet." He tapped the edge of his teacup with his thumb, in time to the music, and smiled. "I'm old and grouchy, I know. But that's nothing new. I've always had the feeling that the children were in charge. Walter used to call them the 'lifers.' Give me someone who knows something I don't. That's my leader. Give me someone like Betsy. Really, if we're going to be honest about it, her talents are wasted around here. She should be someplace where decisions matter. In Turkey. Or China. Maybe if she were in China right now, they'd be at home feeding the masses, instead of chasing the poor Sudanese all over the desert, fighting over scraps."

I was thinking about the redhead as he spoke—her bottom as she knealt over the lettuce, yes, but also the change that came over her when the police car pulled up, as if state interference were a bigger offense than scarcity. "She stared down the police this morning," I said. "And some old bureaucrat too."

"Did she? Yes, they do their dance now and then. The Committee calls it 'the protection of public resources.' Sounds benign enough. In fact, it's just another stupid attempt to remain relevant. They harass us to show us that things are still under their control."

"It's old hat to me. I see it every day back home."

"We hillbillies are only now catching up to your urban futility."

The oatmeal was lukewarm and thickening faster than I could eat it. Soon, the staples would arrive: another gallon of milk, a fresh loaf of bread, sinewy cuts of meat, wilted produce, plenty of nuts. Nate and I would have something nourishing for dinner, and maybe even for lunch. But for breakfast on delivery day, it was a bowl of gelatinous oatmeal, over which Nate had sprinkled some young chives picked from the remains of his kitchen garden. I ate to coat my stomach—which had been gnawing on itself since lunch the previous day—but halfway through the bowl I started to question my decision.

"This really isn't good," I said.

"No. It's awful. I couldn't finish mine, threw it in the bin. But I figured beggars can't be choosers."

He was right. My hunger, once I became aware of it, was overpowering, and I finished my breakfast in one great burst of desperation. Nate watched me with his wallpaper eyes and waited until I was finished. Then he said, "So?"

I thought he meant my father, and I wasn't sure I wanted to discuss George Stark just yet. Nate was smart, articulate, and knew more than I did about my past—and I still wasn't sure I wanted to follow him down that road.

"So what?" I asked.

"So you haven't said anything about the music."

"It's pretty," I said.

"Pretty," he growled. "Pretty's for Easter bonnets and hair bows. The only time music should be pretty is if it's selling something on TV. You'll have to do better than that, now. You're talking to a music critic, William. For the old *Tribune*. For forty years, before everyone stopped caring about such things. Have pity on me now. Humor me and tell me what you hear."

All I could think to say—and this is curious because I'd never used the word before and haven't used it since— was "Eschatology."

His head jerked back as if I'd shot him. "That's a word. Eschatology. My. What is that doing in polite conversation?"

"Just came to me. But it fits, doesn't it?"

"I'm afraid it does. Yes. I was going to say reminiscence, but that amounts to the same thing I suppose."

There were bright tones, bells, chiming, a gathering of energy.

"So you are a music lover then," Nate said.

"Was," I said. "But not this kind."

"Guitars and drums?"

"Mostly."

"The sounds of auto sales, car chases, slasher films."

"I guess."

What remained of a melody faded in a haze of strings and bells, then nothing.

"That was the third movement from an old Adams piece. 'My Father Knew Charles Ives.' It must be decades old by now but I still think of it as new."

"A suggestive title," I said.

"I'm only subtle within limits."

"Really? I hadn't noticed."

"Have you learned anything on that front?"

"Only that my father knew how to tend a vegetable farm."

"He did. Betsy still owes him for that."

V.

After lunch I returned to my father's cabin to shower and change my clothes for the first time in over twenty-four hours. The bathroom was relatively orderly; that is, I found no rotten food on the tile floor and very few loose bullets. Yet the toilet, the sink, and the tub were all ringed with orange minerals and a white film I told myself was soap scum. The dust that had worked its way into me escaped through my pores. As the silt washed out of my hair, I rubbed myself raw. The water frothed a brown foam as it swirled down the drain. But there was too much grime around, and not enough soap left in the world to clean a man bathing in a cesspool. I didn't walk away feeling particularly clean. Some trace of my surroundings clung to me no matter how many times I shampooed.

Cleaner, then, (if not clean) and certainly calmer, I thought about returning to the farm, less to lend a hand than to revisit a new acquaintance. But when I opened the front door and stepped outside—my wet hair combed smooth to my scalp, my chin freshly-shaven—everyone was gone, the redhead included. They'd all run for cover and the fields lay bare in the light of a red afternoon sun, beneath a sky once again blushing in its profound ambivalence, embarrassed by the clouds of poison rolling through on an imperceptible breeze. I closed the door.

Some of what was evil in the air outside had managed to get inside—there had been a great gust when I opened the door—and all of what was rancid inside stayed inside. So my eyes and nostrils were already burning, and my stomach already turning, as I returned to the real work of my stay.

Surveying the wreckage before me, I decided that the only way to proceed was systematically, bureaucratically, by classifying and collating the mounds of debris: bottles by the front door to be discarded; important papers by the couch to be sorted; food wrappers, lottery receipts and assorted trash on the linoleum floor of the kitchenette to be carried out later. A crushed felt Stetson tossed to the side for later consideration. Treasures stashed in the coat closet: a couple of hunting rifles that appeared to be in working order, a crate of CDs (Gordon Lightfoot, Merle Haggard, Emmylou Harris), two leather boots—one chocolate brown, one tan, both for the left foot—and a skillful watercolor of a broad-featured Indian Chief in a feathered headdress, signed "G.S."

I left the tic-tac-toe grid taped to the wall; three x's across the top, three running diagonal from top right to bottom left, the rest o's:

X	X	X
O	X	O
X	O	O

It was a code to be cracked, a mystery saved for another day.

To amuse myself after two hours of tidying, I tried on some of his clothes, whatever didn't smell. Nothing fit. His shirts were overcoats. His pants were windsocks. His belt was at least six sizes too big. But the buckle was a large, rectangular block of tarnished silver, stamped with the image of an angry eagle, wings outstretched, beak open, eye a bead of amber. It was the only thing I found in the cabin that I tucked into my rucksack, to be resized when I returned to the city

Then I slumped back in the arm chair and started reading again:

Certificate of Death

Deceased—Name: Thomas VanBuren Stark
Date of Death: December 13, ----
Age: 71
Date of Birth: May 3, 19--
County of Death: Woodland
City, Town, or Location of Death: Colby
Inside City Limits: Yes
Hospital or Other Institution—Name (If Not In Either, Give Street And Number): Rt. 22, Box 4
Citizen of What Country: USA
Married, Never Married, Widowed, Divorced (Specify): Married
Surviving Spouse (If Wife, Give Maiden Name): Esmeralda Lopez
Usual Occupation (Give Kind of Work Done During Most of Working Life, Even if Retired): Supervisor
Kind of Business or Industry: Agriculture
Residence—State: Alabama
County: Woodland
City, Town, or Location: Colby
Inside City Limits (Specify Yes or No): No
Street and Number: Rt. 22, Box 4

Bavine J. Grass

Woodland County Registrar

Danfield Funeral Home
20 Broad Street P.O. Box 332
Colby, Alabama 32273

Deceased: Mr. William Ray Stark   No. 00-100
Date of Death: April 19, ----   Date of
Statement: April 22,----

Statement of Funeral Goods and Services
Charge for Services Selected:
Transfer of Remains to Funeral Home: from Houston 125.00
Other: Delta Airlines   222.06
          Open and Close Grave   285.00
Traditional Funeral Services Package   1,985.00
Charge for Merchandise Selected:
Casket (or other receptacle): Batesville, J37, Topaz, 18 gauge
steel

                                                 2,790.00
Other Burial Container: Doric Tiara Vault, Fiberglass lined
concrete

                                                 1,065.00
Special Charges
Receiving Remains From: Excelsior Mortuary Svc.   440.00
Cash Advances
Certified Copies of Death Certificate: 6 @ $___each…54.00
Clergy/Musician: Rev. Daniel   25.00
             Rev. Morris   25.00
Summary
Total Funeral Home Charges: 6,912.06
Total Cash Advances: 104.00
Complete Total: 7,016.06
Balance Due: 7,016.06

Clerk of the Courts and County Commission
Eleventh Judicial Circuit
Dade County, Florida

Investigation Witness Account

Witness: State Atty   *Payroll Number 752*   *Days 1*
Miles 33   *Date: 1/26/--*
Amount of Check: 6.98

Pay Exactly 6 Dollars and 98 Cents
For Attendance As A Witness

To The Order of:
George B. Stark
54702 NW 167th Ave
Flatwood, FL 33310

I knew that my patience for the work would be finite, that there would come a day, and soon, when I would be sick of the search, sick of the setting, or just too sick to continue. But for the time being, I was making progress. Thus:

My paternal grandfather, for that was whom I assumed Thomas VanBuren Stark must have been, died in his home in rural Alabama. My uncle and namesake, William Ray Stark, died in Houston. And my father lived somewhere in the vicinity of Miami. At the turn of the century, the Starks were scattered like dandelion seeds. But even if they were scattered, they weren't scattered far enough to be blown away forever. Something had kept them just close enough for death certificates, funerals, and a letter every nine months.

They were a farming family when that was an ignominious thing to be, when anyone who mattered in this world was finding his very own air-conditioned cubicle and hunkering over spreadsheets, to trade, to sell, to provide consultation. Living outside the city limits—and outside Colby "city limits" at that—they weren't even liminal. They were negligible. But that was the irony, because the Starks had actually known things the rest of us were trying desperately to relearn. A good "agricultural supervisor" was becoming harder and harder to find, just when he was needed most. They had missed their chances. Tom with his Latina bride Esmeralda, in a marriage of convenience I'm sure, and certainly not his first or even his second go-around—dying where he lived, at the end of some red clay road in the middle of nowhere. Uncle Billy in Texas, doing who-knows-what, now resting inside two boxes more lavish than any of his residences in life. And George, always in the wrong place at the wrong time, called to testify for or against someone in trouble but refusing to cash the DA's check—out of sheer laziness, or latent radicalism, or maybe even feelings of betrayal and guilt. Or maybe he'd just neglected to open a bank account and had nowhere to take a check once it was received. Three men aimlessly flitting and setting, dying like bugs on a windshield.

My mother told me none of this. She never mentioned anyone named Thomas VanBuren Stark, or Esmeralda Lopez-Stark, or even a William or "Billy," except for me. And she never once mentioned Colby, Alabama. A New Jersey princess to the end, she took special pains to maintain her level of bitterness—blaming my youthful indiscretions on genetics, blaming my B- in high school calculus on "that goddamn laziness you inherited," blaming every overdue bill on "that cockroach and what he's done to us." In response, she pushed the urban virtues, everything that wasn't George Stark or Colby, Alabama. How could she have seen what was coming? How could she have known that only the tradesmen and the "agricultural supervisors" would survive the great decline? How could she have known that I'd be wearing a tool belt full-time before my fortieth birthday—a belt full of tools I didn't know how to use—and wishing that Thomas VanBuren Stark were still around to teach me something to make me useful again in a changed world?

Indeed, if the written record at my feet was in any way representative, Starks were something very like cockroaches. But cockroaches are also survivors:

Hospital Support Service Inc.
P.O. Box 23-11005
Reston, FL 33310

#FFAMKABAKEL
#21859594393#

George B Stark
12A Bleeker Ave.
Flatwood, FL 33310

$7,7590   *CLAIM DATE 6/09/--*
Creditor – S Miami Hospital—Flatwood E/O

THANK YOU FOR YOUR RECENT PAYMENT
FOR YOUR CONVENIENCE, YOU WILL FIND
AN ENVELOPE ENCLOSED FOR YOUR NEXT
PAYMENT

YOUR NEXT DUE DATE IS 11/05/--

Here was proof of real skill, a talent for manipulation that
must have served him well in the difficult times to come. He
was in and out of hospitals for over thirty years. From the
evidence I'd already seen, every collection agent on the
eastern seaboard must have been after him for ambulance
and emergency room fees at one time or another. But they
never managed to tie him down. They barely managed to
find him. And once in a while he threw them a cookie, or
several thousand dollars, and teased them into complacency.
A real cockroach.

But not without his own, peculiar appeal. For here
too was a picture of him from his days in the service, a
younger, thinner version of the man I'd seen in the few
family photographs my mother couldn't bring herself to tear
in half. He was standing in the parade grounds on a military
base, left hand on his hip, bare-chested in fatigue pants and
tall black boots, powerful if not exactly muscular. His blond
curls were flattened to his head in the imprint of a helmet;
his mustache curled in his grin. And between the index and
middle finger of his right hand dangled a cigarette. There
was mischief in this man, posing like a conquering hero
among the white-washed clapboard barracks. Mischief and a
complete lack of foresight.

VI.

Nate overcooked the buffalo steaks but I didn't complain. He also sautéed a head of kale that had been tough enough to remain green through pestilence and drought; resilience was its virtue, and it was still a little sinewy when it reached our plates. Again, no complaints. I was accustomed to windfall and rejects, the bruised and the wilted, the fatty and the grizzled.

He wanted to open a bottle of red wine he'd been saving for over a year and sent me to a kitchen drawer for a corkscrew. I found one buried beneath some wooden spoons, a set of chopsticks, a tangle of rubber bands, and a polished copper bracelet stamped with a caduceus and a red cross.

"You found it," he exclaimed, slipping the bracelet over his green, veiny hand. "I'd like to say I've been looking everywhere for it. It's for my arthritis." He sighed deeply, as if it provided instant relief. "Allow an old man his superstitions, especially if his bones creak every time he moves. Another month of this pain and I was going to start beheading live chickens and spilling their blood on a makeshift altar, if I could find any chickens with heads."

"The hard part these days is to find a chicken with just one head."

We sat at opposite ends of the kitchen table and ate in reverential silence, even ignoring the music until our plates were clear.

"Bach," Nate said then, as we both slid our chairs back from the table, glasses in hand. "Cello Suite number six. There's an arithmetic at work here, and a grace, that no one's ever been able to duplicate. And I mean no one. No higher mathematician, no computer wizard. No one."

Sluggish now with the weight of the first full meal in two days, and heady with bad wine, I listened as if in a delirium, snatching passages from the air as the music stitched through time.

"I always find it's good dinner music," he said, "good on a full stomach. You need a certain preliminary satisfaction, a certain languor before you try to digest something this rich. And you need time to waste for a full appreciation."

"And a glass of wine."

"Or three. Yes." He took another sip and exhaled, contentedly. "Sometimes I think the rationing's a good thing for our souls. Terrible for our constitutions, but good for a modest meal like this one, which wouldn't have been worth our notice in years past. And good for poor Bach, who was having a hard time keeping up with the frenetic pace of modern life until the whole thing came screeching to a halt."

"I thought my education was only to cover the major Americans."

"Consider this a supplement. Sometimes they're all just a little too close anyway."

"The Americans."

"And the moderns. And the postmoderns. And the Romantics. All of them, just a little too close to an old, lonely blind man who needs an escape sometimes." He smiled. "There's no mimicry here. No program. And he never makes a grand show of low aims. A beautiful sound trumps all, thank God. Pure sound. No pandering. It's too late for Bach, of course. Detachment is a luxury we can't afford anymore, at least not for very long. But I miss him, sometimes desperately." He wiped his eyes and drained his glass. "I apologize for old habits. In my mind, I'm always writing the reviews that will never again be published. Never again. Every day I'm a little more certain of that."

"You've heard something?"

"Nothing new. At least nothing surprising. Water reductions for the next two days. And some bad weather on the way, as if it could get worse. Crop predictions that'll give you scurvy. Another slaughter on the subcontinent."

"It wears you down sometimes."

"It does."

I filled his glass, and my own. "Did my father ever talk about his family?"

"You're changing the subject."

"I am."

"Good. Thank you. What do you mean by family?"

"Brothers? Mother and father?"

"Yes, but not in any way I'd consider revealing. Mostly, they came up when he was explaining something, some survival technique he learned from experience. 'The hard way,' as he used to say. Apparently, everything he ever learned he learned 'the hard way.' Poor man. So I heard about how they treated his brother's poison ivy when it got in his ear. How his father planned the rotation of pea plants. How to get help for an accidental gunshot wound without getting the accidental shooter in any sort of accidental legal trouble. How his mother cooked collards. How he and his cousin learned to play guitar without ever knowing the names of the chords. Always practical information. Sometimes he wowed me with what he knew."

"How about my mom?"

"Really?" he asked. "That's what you want to know? Mostly sarcasm. Terrible things, actually, and not very believable. Things said mostly for effect. He loved her till the day he died."

"He said so?"

"I'm an old, blind, widowed fag with erectile dysfunction. All I have left are my intuitions."

"Fair enough. And me?"

"He knew all about you. At least he seemed to. I didn't ask how he found out where you were living, or that you came home from the war without injury. He was very relieved, by the way, but I don't know how he knew any of that."

"Or how we ended up in the same state."

"I guess not. But he mentioned your phone number when he thought he was dying, told me to commit it to memory, and I did."

"Did he ever mention any other children?"

Nate found my eyes, somehow, and stared into them. "Did he have any other children?"

"I don't know."

"You discovered something."

"I don't know."

When the suite was over, Nate selected more Bach, the Goldberg Variations this time. We finished off the bottle. I thought about my morning encounter with Betsy and the redhead and the bureaucrat and the cop. I'd been the only other man in sight. Before the black and white pulled up, I was it. Back home, I was always surrounded by men exactly like me, a great band of displaced, ineffectual men. But here, in Glenden, I was unique somehow, in my prime and living off the bounty of a sad gay widower, a lover of classical music, someone even more obsolete than me.

"I need to give you some money," I blurted out.

"There is no better way to break the spell of Bach than that simple sentence."

"We've never discussed our arrangements. I don't feel right eating your food, drinking your water, using up your rations without repaying you in some way."

"Walter and I had some financial success in our day, and I've been wise with my money. Your presence here is not a burden. Not yet anyway."

"But I need to do something."

"You are here with me. That is something. And you are trying to recover the past, and that is something too. In my opinion, you are doing the only work that matters now."

I left him to his music and walked back to the cabin. It was very dark behind the house, but the moon shone white on the brick walk as I made my way past the thickets and withering vines. Frogs were calling to one another weakly from the trees, but they fell silent as the light found my bare arms. There was a dankness in the heat that night, a swelter hospitable only to amphibians and reptiles, like the snake house at the zoo. And something extra too: a little acid to prick the pores.

Before the siren sounded, I rifled through about a dozen holiday and birthday cards, half of which remained sealed in their colored envelopes, before I spotted a yellowing newspaper clipping, undated, peaking out from the bottom of a pile. Beneath a headline reading "Snapshots" was a photo of my mother holding a pistol, aiming across the page, left to right. Beside her, facing the camera, was a soldier in fatigues and sunglasses. In the background, the scene was repeated twice more—woman aiming, soldier advising—in a line that ran out of the frame. My mother's hair was buzzed short, so I knew it was taken during her cancer days, close to the end, during the run-up to the war. She looked so resolute before her fate, with her jaw set and her eyes narrowed, blinking down the barrel of a gun she must have hated with every ounce of civility left in her bony frame:

A local handgun safety review committee met Friday morning at the firing range behind the Deerfield Police Headquarters to learn about the power of handguns. In the foreground, Laura Guarino, of Ridgefield, receives guidance from Lt. Henry Haring, of the 98th Division, Army Reserves. Also pictured are Mary Nixon, Sgt. Robert Walsh, Lt. Joseph Weiss, and Lisa Steele. Steele said members of the committee decided to meet at the firing range "to build awareness (for handguns) that would make us better evaluators of the program." The handgun safety review committee was formed in cooperation with the National Guard, Steele said.

What a surprise it must have been for George Stark to come across his ex-wife in the newspapers, posing as part of the homeland mobilization. What a surprise it was for me now to see what she was doing in those final days and to find that it was almost exactly what I had been doing. At opposite ends of the country, both of us were training our eyes, getting acquainted with the weight and balance of death in our hands.

I stared at the photo for what seemed like hours. Then came lights-out, mercifully. But I didn't even try to sleep. I sat by the front window—which I'd scrubbed and which was now partially translucent—and watched the moonlight drag along the fields below. I held the clipping in my hand as I'd held on to my draft notice years earlier. It was stuck to my hand, or I was stuck to it, as the fields changed slowly with the hours. Undisturbed by wind or breeze, they shifted with the rotation of the earth and the sidelong glances of a pale light.

Just when my mind began to drift, something caught my eye: a sudden rustling beginning in the fallow grasses, first ripples and then a tide swaying the tall stalks, deliberate and sure.

At first, I thought it was the wine showing me visions. But the figures had substance and moved in nervous fidgets. They began gliding up and down the crop rows, covering every inch of the field, humans certainly, but oddly-shaped, angular and indistinct. They scurried, stopped, and scurried on like mice in a maze. I stood with my hands pressed to the glass, my breathing visible and rapid under my nose as I strained for a clear view. Something was happening, but I couldn't tell what it was.

I fell asleep soon after the shadows returned to the darkness, and dreamed that I was on my way to the front again.

VII.

What happened next may not have happened at all.

At some point during the night—it could have been hours after I fell asleep, it could have been ten minutes, it could have been a dream—I woke with a start to an impatient knocking at the door and a voice calling in a high whisper: "*Open up. It's me you son of a bitch. Come on already, open the goddamn door.*" I tried to remain perfectly still, to make no sound, but the knocking grew louder and the voice, not Nate's, became more desperate. "*It's me, goddamn it. Don't leave me out here.*" He was pounding with both fists now, shaking the door, the wall, the window rattling in its frame. "*Stark, you bastard.*" I lurched out of the chair, tripped over something I couldn't see, and fell to the floor. "*I hear you stumbling around in there, you clumsy shithead.*" I ran for the closet, grabbed one of the rifles—it didn't matter which, all were unloaded—then inched to the front door with my back to the wall the way the besieged always do in movies, and not quite the way I'd been trained to do it in boot camp.

I reached out and unlocked the door; the click was as loud as a gunshot. Turning the knob as slowly and quietly as I could, I took one last deep breath before I threw open the door and pointed the muzzle of the rifle into the face of a man in a hooded sweatshirt. He had pulled the hood over his head and drawn the strings so tightly that only his nose stuck out in the fading moonlight, an awkward finger of exposed white flesh. A head like a pea in a pod, and a nose, and a body hidden under many layers.

He was standing perfectly still. I kept the rifle trained on his nose, but he did not flinch. Arms at his sides, he waited for my next move.

I had no next move. After a while, he seemed to realize it.

"Stark home?" he asked.

"No."

"Expect him home soon?"

"No."

"Well, if you see him, can you tell him Jimmy stopped by?"

"Any other message?"

"No. Just wanted to see what he was up to."

"Okay."

"Have a good night."

He hobbled away like an old dog with a hurt paw, shuddering with every step. He was half way into the woods and coughing before I lowered the rifle and closed the door. After a while, my heart stopped racing and I fell asleep again.

Or else I'd never been awake in the first place.

VIII.

Up at sunrise, I didn't have the stomach to start on the scrap pile again. I just sat and waited for something else to grab my attention, like Betsy's little gray car rolling to a stop on the gravel square beside the greenhouse.

She was dragging crates of hand tools along the ground when I walked up. Her skin was red from the heat and strain, even redder against the strands of white hair that fell from her straw hat every time she wrenched a crate a little closer to the sheds. It was worrisome to see her this way, twisting awkwardly—an ill omen for an enterprise that didn't need another ill omen.

"I can take that for you," I said.

Her first look was savage. She hadn't heard me approach and her eyes flashed a combination of fear and hatred. She even bared her teeth. But then she softened. "Oh it's you," she said. "George's son. I waited for you yesterday but you never came back."

"Sorry about that. I was attending to other matters."

"I understand. How's it going over there? You sorting through your dad's stuff? I bet there's a lot."

"There is."

"There would be. George didn't even clean up after himself when he came around here. Always a pair of gloves and some apple peels where he was sitting. Loved his fruit, the sweeter the better, and what he didn't eat, he'd whittle. Once he gave me a teddy bear made out of pear." She smiled and dusted the front of her shirt. "Well, I sure can use your help today, if you're here to offer it. The ladies won't be coming. They're spread so thin, they can only work a few days a week. But the crops don't seem to understand their schedule."

"Never any men?"

She squinted into the early sun and studied my face for the first time, looking for some sign of my disability. "You haven't gotten out much have you?"

"Not since I've been here."

"But you watch the news?"

"Before I got here."

"So you know about widow towns?"

"I do."

"Well this is one of them. A 'demographic anomaly.' When the trouble started, everyone with a penis enlisted and ran off to Mexico half-cocked, so to speak, and very few of them came home. We're missing a whole generation of our boys, and quite a few of our girls."

I had a prepared statement for situations like this and had mastered its delivery through countless repetitions. But it sounded so hollow this time that I regretted saying anything at all. "I was on my way to the front when the armistice was signed. We were actually in a transport, rolling through Arizona, when we turned around and came home."

She nodded and waved me off. "No need to explain. I'm glad you're here."

She told me to stack the crates in the shed and then to meet her at the far corner of the field by the leaf pile. Some minutes later I found her at the end of a long walkway a few feet into the tree line, studying some apiaries half buried in brush. She was fanning herself with her hat but visibly cooking inside her denim and boots. Her head was listing forward, her chin nearly touching her sternum, and her collar was already stained with sweat. Together, we watched a single black speck fly out of a hole in the side of one of the towers, slam into the wall above the hole, and then right itself and buzz over our heads.

"Damn bees aren't keeping up their end of the bargain," she said. "The whole population collapses every few years now, and it looks like this is going to be one of those years. They're all dopey."

"What can we do about that?"

"That's the million dollar question. I don't suppose you have the right organ for pollination. Don't answer that. All we can do is do what we can. So let's get to work. You ever mulch before?"

"No."

"All it means is you drop leaves around the plants to keep the water in the ground and the weeds out. Got it? You have to pile them up at least an inch thick, more if you have enough leaves. We've had so little rain there aren't even many weeds to pull just yet, but if you find any, pull them out and drop them where you find them. Now I seem to remember you working in the carrots yesterday, right? Be especially gentle around those. There's a wheelbarrow on the other side of the pile, and there should be a pitchfork stuck in the back somewhere."

"Okay."

"And thanks."

I rolled up my sleeves and dug in. The mulch pile was oily and squamous, flaking off in layers as I forked it; broad, flat leaves in the first foot or so, crumbly fragments for the next two feet, and then a sludgy, steaming compost compressed to the ground. I started on the peas with the first full wheelbarrow. The tendrils were just beginning to snag the guide strings and stakes, just beginning to find their vertical paths, and I made quick work of them, heaping mulch in mounds beneath their lowest limbs. To my surprise, this kind of thing came easily to me, as if I'd inherited a skill from a band of Alabama nomads. I found that I enjoyed this work more than I enjoyed working construction, or roofing, or any of the other odd jobs I'd picked up in recent years, at which I remained forever a novice. This work made sense to me: it was modest—I was moving leaves from one place to another—but it wasn't wasteful or futile. And it was physical, which was a relief after spending a couple of days cooped up in the compound with Nate. The sun cut sharply through a smoky haze and I knew I'd have to take cover soon, but while I was working I was able to stop thinking.

I finished the pea rows and two of the carrot rows—cutting deep enough into the leaf pile to find three or four pockets of fat, pink earthworms—until the sun made me too dizzy to continue. Then I dropped my tools and took cover with Betsy, whom I found stretched out in the narrow shade behind the shed, her hat on the ground, her head against the shingles, her red face now gray and dripping.

"You okay?"

"I'm fine," she said. "Just time for a break is all. I'm old and this is what happens. First you're weeding a bed of lettuce, then you're wondering how the sun got so close, and then it's too late and the sun's sitting right on your shoulder."

"Can I get you some water?"

"Had some. How are you doing?"

"Fine, until I wasn't fine anymore."

"That's it. That's what it's like." She wiped the sweat from her forehead and took a deep, halting breath like a child after a fit of sobbing. "Did you notice anything odd out there? Anything unusual today?"

I shrugged. "To me, everything looks odd out there."

"Where are all the birds? Not a chirp. Not a tweet. Definitely no songbirds. I haven't heard a songbird around here in months. Maybe a year. And this place used to be full of them. But forget them. I haven't even seen a single goddamn cardinal in months. Or a blue jay, and I hate blue jays, but I'd sure like to see a blue jay now."

"I'm ashamed to say I didn't notice that there were no birds."

"Isn't that sad? That a smart guy like you wouldn't notice?"

"Embarrassing."

"That tree over there, that crabapple used to produce the tartest, knottiest little fruits you ever ate. You couldn't eat a whole one, they were so tart. And there used to be a nest of orioles buried in there, birds of an orange color no one's ever been able to reproduce. When one of those orioles flew out of that tree, everyone used to stop what they were doing and watch. No matter what you were doing, you had to watch. It was like the gods were skywriting."

"It's a beautiful place," I said, just to have said something. In fact, it had been a beautiful place once upon a time, but it wasn't anymore.

"Ah," Betsy replied, waving her hand as if she would level it all for the right price. "It's a goddamn piece of real estate, and the real estate market's dead. Otherwise I'd sell it for condominiums. It's worthless. Soon enough this whole plot will be covered in knotweed."

"You're done for the day?"

"You can't work in this kind of light. Look at the glare. That'll tear right through your clothes. There's not enough sunscreen in the world to protect you from that."

"I'm sorry you're not getting more help."

"You were more help today than I've gotten in a while."

"I'll be back tomorrow."

"Good."

"Does everyone come back tomorrow?"

"My widows. Yes."

I wanted to ask about the redhead specifically but I couldn't bring myself to press Betsy about her. Dignity revolted against an active pursuit. Widowed and mourning was more forbidding to me than happily married. The soldiers' code. *"On behalf of a grateful nation."*

"I almost forgot," Betsy said, her face pink once more, if not yet the usual red. "Take these to Nate." She threw a clutch of green into my arms, a bouquet of thick, odd-looking succulents with reddish stems and small leaves.

"What's this?"

"That's purslane. It's a weed, and a real bastard. It takes over entire beds of less hearty plants, elbows them right out. But it's more nutritious than lettuce. I'm always fighting this stuff, but it may be our bumper crop this year, so I figure we may as well go with it. Nate will know what to do with it."

"Thanks I guess."

"Don't thank me until you taste it."

IX.

"Thoreau ate it. That's what Walter always said when he was cooking it up." Nate's hands were quick and sure with the knife. He sliced the roots away, trimmed some of the thicker stems, then chopped the branches and leaves into a pan coated with hot oil and a little garlic powder. "I find I have to repeat his favorite phrases from time to time, so I don't lose them."

"Walter's."

"Right. Thoreau's too, I suppose. But I mean Walter's. I have to keep saying them out loud. It's how I know where I am."

He stirred the pan with a wooden spoon. The leaves sizzled and spit, and the hot oil pricked his hand. He bit his palm, cursed, then stirred again. "That kind of information used to matter more than it does today. 'Thoreau ate it.' It certainly mattered to Walter, and it's come to mean something to me in my old age. It still gives me comfort to know that one of our few, true geniuses gave this horrible plant his endorsement. I'm sure he ate many things we'd consider beneath us, even now. But I still trust his opinion enough to feel self-righteous about things like weeds, and superior to anyone who's never eaten purslane. Maybe that's what genius is after all, trustworthy opinions."

"Ever the critic," I said.

"Precisely."

"Well, it looks like seaweed to me."

"It does. Land kelp. Tastes a little like seaweed too, which is to say that it isn't entirely awful. In fact, if I didn't know it was a weed, I'd quite like it. But then I've always had a fondness for rejects. You should have seen Walter." He smiled. "Walter was a weed in every garden but mine."

He'd given me a tall glass of water without ice—he said I'd cool down faster if I didn't freeze my system—and sat me at the dark end of the kitchen beneath a hanging basket spilling over with dusty, crumbling hydrangea flowers.

"Sit in the shadows for a while," he said, "and give the heat stroke some time to reconsider." He wasn't playing any music now, which was fortunate for me. My head had been hollowed out by the sun and was echoing everything, even the blood running in my veins. I sipped the water, braced myself against a cataract roar, and waited for a restoration which came slowly and then all at once, until I was able to stand beside him again and watch him finish preparing my lunch.

"You like it here," he said.

"How do you mean?"

"The absurd pace of this place. It suits you. You go down to the fields. You work as hard as you can for as long as you can. Then you come back, eat a little something, and continue your pursuit of things profound and petty."

"I hadn't thought of that," I said, though I didn't say he wasn't right.

"There's an economics to it that agrees with you and your constitution. You know, if I'm not mistaken, I'd even say that you have a little of Thoreau in you."

I liked the sound of that. It brought to mind happy associations of my youth, the reading and the aspiration that the subsequent twenty years had done their best to choke— literally to choke out of me.

"We're in such disarray," I said after a long pause. "We've been waiting for so long for whatever's coming next that we've gotten sloppy. I've gotten sloppy. I don't know what I've been thinking. That everything would turn around and that there'd suddenly be a place for me again? In the last few years, I've been on every work-crew in the city. I've helped to rebuild everything that's actually been rebuilt. I have absolutely no skill in this line of work, but I've done it to the best of my ability and paid my dues and bided my time, believing that it all had to come around again. Back to normal. That hope alone was my payment, and kept me going without complaint. But we have to be honest with ourselves at some point. We have to admit that the time for what…for satisfaction, that time may never come around again.”

“No. Not the way it was.”

“So then it’s…it’s time for me to get real.”

Nate smiled as he divided the sautéed greens onto two plates and handed me one.

“Not an easy thing for me, getting real.”

“No,” he said. “You’re a dreamer.”

“That’s what my mother always said. In another life, I’d have been a full-blown optimist.”

“So you’re staying?”

“I don’t know what I’m doing, but I do know I have to figure it out soon. If I wait any longer, it’ll be too late.”

“This is a very interesting speech,” Nate said then. “I live the last few years incommunicado, basically in silence, except for a few words exchanged here and there with delivery boys, the remaining neighbors, the farm ladies, your father. A hermit in a house full of ghosts I can’t even see. And then you come in here this afternoon and deliver a rousing speech. Very interesting how some things do turn around.”

He couldn’t see me blush, and for that I was grateful. I filled my mouth full of the weed—inoffensive, even tasty with proper seasoning, a little slimy—and hoped the moment would pass. But I had a lump in my throat now, goosebumps, a new and ill-defined excitement, an urge to scream until I’d emptied my lungs.

“This isn’t bad,” Nate said to himself as he scooped a forkful into his mouth. He leaned against the counter as he ate, holding his plate beneath his chin. “I haven’t completely lost my touch.” Then he looked at my shoulder and his face tightened with the import of what he was about to say. “Don’t you even think about being embarrassed. Speeches like yours will keep us alive.”

I nodded, inanely, and continued eating.

X.

The afternoon was gathering a new virulence as I walked back to my father's cabin. Beneath suicide gray skies hung a fetid odor, close and warm, like the smell of a public health clinic—the smell of sickness and of vermin in the leaves. On its way was another evening for two-ply masks and a half bottle of eye drops.

Something had been foraging in the old gardens; there were budless stems along the edges and headless dandelions growing through the slate walkway. A single yellow bloom appeared beneath a shapeless boxwood; all else was closely-cropped, decapitated, uniform.

I heard a rustle of paper over my right shoulder, turned in time to see a proud little robin fly past my ear and light on a rock, his breast a dim brown but his eye sharp and his head quick, pivoting in search of family, or food, or cover. I whispered a sad greeting, knowing that I would outlive him and, very likely, his entire species. I'd be able to lock myself inside my father's cabin and wait out the poison while he would end the night gasping, landed and alone. I thought I heard him chirp after me as I opened the front door but he was gone when I looked back. Only the dead moss, the color of his breast, remained on the rock.

Earlier that morning, I'd set aside a small stack of papers to sort through later, things that appeared to be of particular interest. I sat on the couch now and tried to focus.

When I awoke, a sharp pain tore through my head, a flash so hot I thought I'd been mugged in my sleep. I sat for a long time until the pain lost its edge and left me to my cotton mouth and my paradoxically full bladder. Physical labor, prolonged exposure, a limited diet, rationed water…and I had a hangover. A guilt-free hangover, the worst kind. I felt my way to the bathroom and pissed a copious, noisome solution. Then I shuffled back to the living room, falling this time onto the dry armchair beside

the picture window, where I rubbed my face with my
blistered hands and tried to ward off the coming fantasias of
insomnia.

Of course I'd been here before, awake and alone in
the wee hours when my aimlessness, my dreamlessness,
turned into something morbid and accusatory—a
consciousness of clenched fists and halitosis; minor erections
and intestinal distress. Here I was again, and it was lonelier
than I remembered.

The moon dipped behind the trees to the west so
that the light radiated without glare, as if filtered through
bones and gauze. In the eastern sky, the blackout had
yielded a blizzard of stars. I sat in that chair for what could
have been hours but was more likely about twenty minutes,
and thought about nothing but astronomy—distance
measured in light, time measured in physics, existence
plotted against a vacuum. There were other worlds out
there, after all, even if they weren't mine.

And that's when I saw them again: the cones of
white light circling the ground and the shadows creeping
close behind. Sometimes the flashes were focused on
particular plants or patches of treacherous terrain; sometimes
they swung across wide swaths of ground and danced across
the dark expanse.

The figures, more than five but I could not tell how
many more, scampered like children. Their shadows veered
and swerved and righted themselves, stumbled across the
field, slumped in small heaps, collapsed after great exertion.
Their efforts were targeted, deliberate, but something about
them was awry and wayward and I wondered what they were
carrying, what weight burdened them, pitched them from
side to side like rickety freight cars.

Torn between a possessive impulse to reclaim the
farm for its rightful owners, and a sinking feeling of regret
that anyone in a place like Glenden could be reduced to
scavenging in the middle of the night, I watched them with
both hands pressed to the glass, my breath clouding my view

once more. Weeds, I thought. Pick the weeds but leave the crops. I almost went down to warn them. But before I could turn toward the door, all the beams of flashlight jerked simultaneously, scattered across the field in different directions, and were extinguished. A police car skidded to a halt at the roadside, then nosed ten or twenty feet into the field and shined its headlights into the emptiness where they had been only seconds before.

I made up my mind to be happy that no one was caught.

XI.

I woke a second time that night to the smell of ozone and a rage of lightning. Some flashes struck soundlessly; some accompanied the sharp cracking of splitting trees. Some were chased by the hollow roar of the thunder, the loudest sound I'd heard since the war. I dropped to the floor once in post-traumatic fear. Then came the deluge.

The storm was over by daybreak, but everything was still bated and anxious as the sun rose again. I walked down to the farm at the first brightening to inspect the muddy rows where they had been the night before, searching for their footprints, for signs of their intrusion. Any trace had been washed away during the storm. The plants were sodden and drooping, but they seemed otherwise unharmed. In fact, I observed no loss, nothing ravaged, nothing changed in the eighteen hours since Betsy and I had run for cover—which was a puzzle to me. The men had been there, and so had the storm, but neither had left a lasting impression. Just the water soaking through my jeans to my ankles.

Chilled for the first time in weeks, I strolled through the small greenhouse to warm up. Inside the plastic-roofed Quonset—dripping along its seams, as humid as a cave—were two rows of long wooden tables supporting dozens of seedling flats. From each flat poked a popsickle stick neatly labeled with the variety of plant now sprouting. By the look of things, the second wave of planting was healthier than the first. In their ice-cube cups, new lettuces and parsleys were greener and more promising than their vigorless counterparts in the fields, and there were so many plants lined up so evenly, in such straight, tidy rows, that I could almost begin to imagine better days a'comin'.

"What do you think?" Betsy asked.

Startled, I jumped a few inches off the wood planking floor. She laughed and brushed by me carrying a garden hose wrapped over her shoulders.

"Deceptive, isn't it?" she said. "Everything looks so good in here. A few hours in that sun, however."

"The storm woke me up and I couldn't get back to sleep so I came down and took a look around."

"No need to explain," she said, dropping the hose she was carrying on a pile of hoses in the near corner. "I trust you. Maybe I shouldn't, but I do. Besides, it's nice in here in the morning, cozy. But I defy you stand in here at noon."

"Gonna be a cooker today, I take it."

"That's what I hear. But what else is new, really. Any trees down around Nate's?"

"Two in the woods behind the house, and a young one by the back porch. Fortunately, no damage to the house."

"That old man must have a horseshoe up his butt, he's so lucky. Or else he's got a special kind of help." She winked at me and ran her hand along the tops of the plants, petting them. I nodded as if I understood. "Yes, it was some storm. I'll take the rain, though. God knows it wasn't enough, but I'll take what I can get."

"Will it make any difference at all?"

"Cross fingers."

"What happens if it doesn't?"

Betsy shrugged, rolled her eyes. She couldn't afford to think too long about hypotheticals. "Everyone goes back to the supermarket and buys what little they can with what little they have, and our problems, big and small, continue to multiply."

"That's what's gonna happen, isn't it?"

"Yep. That's what's gonna happen. Eventually. Sooner than later."

"So what can I do today?"

Weeding. Purslane dropped in big, white painter's buckets to be distributed to the widows. Everything else uprooted and left where it was found, to be trampled to dust between the beds as a foothold for farmers and a mulch barrier to other weeds. Later, Betsy showed me the difference between beneficial insects and parasitic beetles, and set me to picking the latter from the bottoms of potato leaves, squeezing their larvae and the heads of adults between my fingertips, a task I hated but performed as any good soldier would.

This was my job, insect executioner, when the widows trickled in with their children in tow and got to work. Once again they kept their voices low but soon filled the quiet of the fields with a welcome hum. And their return seemed to encourage other living things to come out of hiding as well, because the dragonflies were soon zipping overhead and I even noticed a butterfly or two fluttering in the heat, having struggled all this way north for milkweed only to find that they had further still to go.

She came over to me this time, her red hair pulled back and her eyes enormous. She was the prettiest thing I'd seen in days, and I felt the old twist in my gut as she approached. For a moment I was genuinely happy to find something I thought I'd lost.

"You're here again," she said.

"Surprised?"

"I am. Men come by once in a while, but this farm's such a henhouse they usually get scared away."

"I guess I don't have too much regard for most of the men I meet these days," I said, laughing. "I prefer the henhouse."

She smiled, but I could see that I had caused her a little pain.

"The truth is," I said, serious now and hoping to regain her trust, "I think I can help here in a way I wasn't able to help back home."

"What did you do?"

"You mean professionally? Well, I'm useless by training and vocation. So I've been working in the trades since the war."

She smiled again, this time with real humor, and pulled a branching clover out of the ground, roots and all. "What does it mean to be useless?"

"It means I was preparing for a literary life."

"Reporter? Editor? What?"

"I wasn't quite sure which way I was going when I dropped the whole idea."

"I can see that." She sat up and looked at my face, at my chin and forehead. Her eyes were appraising, taking me in. "Things took a less than literary turn." She wiped a drop of sweat from her freckled nose. "Where were you stationed?"

"I was headed to the front when the armistice was signed."

She nodded. "I'm sorry," she said.

No one had ever said that to me. It was an extraordinary thing for her to say. It meant that she was allowing my guilt to kneel—if not comfortably, then at least openly—beside her mourning. She was acknowledging that her husband's death and my inaction were both circumstances beyond control, and it cleared the air between us. It freed us to talk like friends.

"I'm Will, by the way."

We shook hands. "Laura."

"So how is everyone getting on?" I asked.

She pulled a few more weeds then dusted her hands on her lap. "You mean my family? My daughter's one of those wild, scrawny beasts in the trees over there. My son's at school. We're getting by." She paused to consider how much more she wanted to tell me. When she tightened her lips, a dimple appeared on her cheek, beside the mole, among the freckles. Hers was a busy sort of beauty. I liked her even more because she wasn't simple. "I have some relatives nearby, and I've been able to do some part-time work as needed, temping locally, at Town Hall, putting my own four-star education to good use. So we manage. My daughter has the cough, and that's a concern, and I've noticed that my son won't watch television anymore. I guess he's afraid that he'll hear more bad news, though I can't imagine what could be worse than the news he's already received." She caught my eye. "That's how he found out about his dad. The name appeared on one of those lists and he saw it before I could change the channel. So now I have a third grader who won't watch TV and a preschooler showing some early symptoms." Her eyes were sad, sad but hard, as if she were daring me to have an opinion about her life story. "And for all that, we're still better off than many I know. At least we still have a safety net."

"Parents?"

"His. And some cousins too. We're closer now than we were before the war. Those relationships haven't faded yet. They will, I know. We'll drift apart as we get used to this, and return to our separate corners, which will be a relief in some ways. But for now we're sticking to our story that we're all a great comfort to each other, and good friends in the short term." She smiled and shrugged her shoulders. I wanted to do something simple and sweet for her. I wanted to hold her hand.

"As I said before, I admire your strength. Whether you want me to or not."

"Not just mine. Look around. We're all here for the same reason. You too."   "My situation's a little different. I didn't really come here to join an effort to rebuild civilization. I was called here by a man I'd never met before, who told me that my father, another man I'd never met before, had just died and would I like to come by and look through my father's stuff."

"The blind guy up there? He called you?"
"Yep."
"So your father was the scary guy? George?"
"That's what I'm told."

"Unbelievable. You couldn't be more different."

"You don't find me scary?"

"Sorry, no."

"What was he like?"

"George was big and slow and very polite. Don't get me wrong. He was very nice to everyone. But he was always around, you know? You'd go to the greenhouse and he was there. He was in the shed. He'd crawl out of the woods when you passed by. It was like there were twenty of him. Twenty big, slow Georges hiding in every shadow. And every time he appeared I'd squeal like a little girl. He scared me every time."

"Weird."

"I hope you don't mind me telling you this."

"Not at all. I asked."

"Well, it was weird. Big, slow guy like that always sneaking around. And all these women and children only half paying attention. He never did anything wrong, of course."

"But he was creepy."

"Thank you. Yes. Creepy."

"I've been coming to the same conclusion," I said. "It's a bit worrisome to find out that your father was a little creepy, or a lot creepy. But here's how I've been thinking about it, and you tell me if I'm creepy too." I was making it all up on the spot; I'd have said or done just about anything to make her smile again. "Genetics are working in my favor. If you cross a male donkey and a female horse, you get a mule, which is a useful, if stupid, beast of burden. But if you cross a female donkey and a male horse, you get a hinny, which, I'm told, is a completely useless animal. Well, from everything I've learned, daddy was the donkey in my family. I know my mother was a thoroughbred. So it could have been worse for me."

Her laughter was deep and a little nervous. "You know," she said, "You're right. You're a little creepy too."

I brayed and she laughed again. "So what have you learned?" she asked.

I picked a pair of fornicating beetles from the underside of a leaf and squeezed them together until they made a sickening crunch. This is what I've learned, I thought to myself. I've learned to read the small detail and extrapolate—a Biblical plague from the copulation of a couple of insects, a coming revolution from a couple of hobos fleeing through a field at night, an entire man from an unpaid ambulance bill. Redemption in a vanishing dimple.

"A little," I said. "You really want to hear this?"

"What else do we have to talk about?"

"Good point. So, let's see. My father, George Stark, got off to a bad start. Poor rural kid joins the military, comes home and starts a family, then loses his job and climbs into a bottle. Or maybe it was other way around. Either way, it's nothing too surprising. A good ole boy too lazy for adulthood and not resilient enough to face down misfortune. A dime a dozen. Two things bother me, however. First, I don't know how he or Nate, the blind guy up there, ever found me, since everyone I've ever known lost track of my father twenty years ago. And second, I found a weird reference in a letter, but only one, to my father's kids, plural, and I grew up an only child. At least I thought I did."

"Wow. So there are mysteries. Kind of exciting. Any leads?"

Her eyes were wide now and she was smiling without hesitation. Clearly, she'd had her fill of hard information and cold fact, and my story offered very little of either.

"Nothing, but there's still a pile of paper to sort through. My father left me an absolute mess."

"It's not really a mystery, though, him finding you. I mean, we've all left a trail."

"I don't get the sense that he was ever really plugged-in. I can't even imagine him typing. Besides, if it's been this easy for people like us to reenter the Dark Ages, how much easier must it have been for an old drunk and even older blind man to go primitive at the first sign of inconvenience?”

“I don’t know how easy it’s been for any of us,” she said, her face turned away from me now, her shoulder moving slowly between us. “It wasn’t our choice, was it? Conversations were interrupted. Address books emptied out. If there’s nothing to buy and no one to talk to, what’s the point, right? But your father still had a reason.”

“I hadn’t thought of that,” I said. I tried to imagine a somewhere out there where commerce and communication all continued apace, where bytes of information were still traveling through the air, documenting it all, documenting me even as I had my hands in the dirt, even as I stooped to squash a beetle between my fingertips. And I couldn’t imagine it; I couldn’t imagine a place where everyone hadn’t already powered down and walked away.

“I don’t know.” I looked up at Nate’s house, broad-shouldered and stately on the hill, and my father’s cabin beside it, peaking out from behind a tree. “George Stark lived his whole life on little scraps of paper.”

She sat back on her heels, pushed the hair from face, and looked at me with a puzzled expression, as if I’d begun speaking in tongues. For a moment, I wondered if I had, so abruptly did I lose her interest. But then she held her forearm to her brow, shaded her eyes, and cursed under her breath. Other women around us began to groan as well. Only then did I hear the cars returning.

The first two were police cars, one officer in each. The third was a brown sedan out of which climbed three older men, one gray and balding, one just gray, both a little portly in jeans and shirtsleeves, and the man called David, the aging show-pony in the baseball cap who had visited us two days earlier. Flanked by the officers, the three bureaucrats marched down the middle of the field to Betsy, who took off her straw hat, wiped her brow with the back of her wrist, and met them nose to nose.

"This is it," the bald man said, as if he were continuing an ongoing conversation, as if Betsy were expecting him. "We just got the word. We can't let this go on any longer."

"Can't let what go on, John?" Betsy asked.

"We need production in every quarter. Production, Betsy. It's time to force the issue."

She took a deep, librarian's breath of infinite patience and said, "I've explained this before, John. I know we haven't produced much but this is still the growing season. Not the harvest season. You know the difference, right? Let me simplify it for you. It's like Thanksgiving, which celebrates the harvest after months of privation. That's a fall holiday, John, which makes these the months of privation. You have to let things grow in the spring before you pick them in the fall, and you really can't make them grow any faster than they want to. So why don't you be a good little pilgrim and run along until we natives come calling."

"We can speed this up and you know it."

"John. You're a bald little man. The sun's gotta be murder on that scalp of yours. If you're not smart enough to wear a hat, you're not smart enough to run a farm."

"That's very funny."

"Screw funny!" Betsy shouted. "How the hell do you think things got this bad in the first place? Why is that sun burning away what little is left of your brain? Because we let people like you run things. You miserable little..."

"It's too late," the gray-haired man said then, reaching out and touching Betsy's shoulder.

"What?" she asked, pushing him away.

"It's too late. We can't wait for everything to turn around. We all understand that's the ideal, and we've given it a try, but it's just not feasible in the timeframe we're working with. We need to start getting something out of this place. There are just too many people out there, Betsy. The demand is too high. Good intentions aren't enough to feed them all."

She looked at David, who was looking down at his feet, his face shielded by the bill of his cap. He clutched his hands behind his back and toed a clod that had already dried to powder.

"So this is a new policy, then," she said, exhaling again, this time in resignation.

"State wide."

"So we're giving up."

"Everything's against us, Betsy. Even the air is against us now. The right way is, for all intents and purposes, the wrong way for us now."

"Time to ship in the chemicals."

"Yes."

"And continue what you've started."

"Yes."

Betsy saw that we were listening and she smiled weakly, her eyes shrinking, withdrawing into her rapidly-aging face. "Wonderful," she said. "So what are you gonna do with me?"

"We'd like you to stay on for the transition."

"And my friends here?" She was still looking at us; to my surprise, she was looking at me most of all, as if we understood each other and were concocting a plan telepathically. But all I could think about was how satisfying it would be to spear one of them through the chest with a pitchfork.

"I'm not quite sure yet. We'll have to see how the new program works and whether it reduces the need for volunteers."

"It won't work, you know." She turned back to the men again. "Maybe you'll feed a few more people for a little while, but you won't be able to sustain this place for long. I'm the long-term solution if there is one, and you know it."

The bald man folded his arms and huffed, but the gray-haired man nodded and David said, softly, "That's what

I told them." He raised his eyes just long enough to squint at Betsy before resuming his inspection of the depleted soil at his feet.

Laura and I walked to Betsy's side.

"I'm sorry everyone," the gray-haired man said now in a voice that carried across the wilting plants. Over his head I could see a front moving in along the tree line, purple clouds as dense and folded as paper maché. Shrewdly, these men had gotten from us all they could before the weather sent us home. "The municipality has decided to restructure the business model of this farm and others like it in anticipation of a long, hard summer. What we'd like is for you to drop what you're doing and take the rest of the day off." Dozens of people appeared now in the surrounding rows, women working through the aches and pains of stoop labor, lower backs unlocking, knees giving way then stiffening, necks creaking as they turned—a whole field sprouting humans like so many feeble plants. "We'll get back to you in a few days to explain the new structure and outline the new work requirements."

Betsy waited until he seemed satisfied with his explanation. Then she stepped forward and shoved the gray-haired man aside. "What they're really doing is reversing our practices," she called out. "The short term gains will be obvious. You will take home more food in the coming months than you would have otherwise. But the system will break down in other ways, and next year you'll have much bigger problems than you do right now." She took off her hat again and wiped her brow. "It's goddamn hot out here and those clouds look treacherous. You'll probably need your masks tonight, if you're dumb enough to go outside. But get used to it, because there's more on the way."

"You overstate the dangers. Our best predictions indicate…"

Betsy grabbed the front of the bald man's shirt. "How many quarters do you oversee?"

He looked startled, then angry, but answered anyway. "Four."

"Good, John. That's right. You have four quarters. And you're doing this to each of them?"

"We are."

"And how much crap do you plan to dump on all this real estate to get it producing again?"

"I can't give you a hard figure yet. We have people…"

"Times four, right John?"

"I'm sure there are variations, but we expect that all four farms will require approximately the same attention. Yes."

"That's a great big pile of crap, John, because the soil is tired and abused. And all that crap will head straight for the groundwater the first time it rains. And even you understand that the rest of this system will collapse under all that weight, maybe even by the end of the summer. That's how fragile things are now."

"What do you propose we tell all of these mothers when your farm doesn't produce the essentials for their kids? Iron, vitamins."

"Roughage, right John?"

"Where is it all, Betsy?" He swept his arm over our pitiful efforts.

"Tell them what I always tell them, John. That it's going to take a long time to repair the damage you caused."

"That's it? Blame us and be patient? That's all you have?"

"Here they are, John. My widows. Ask them if they understand what they've signed up for. Ask them if they understand hardship."

He caught his breath. "This is pointless. We've already weighed all the options and the decision has been made. We're duty-bound to take over."

"Do your duty," Betsy said and headed for the sheds. "I'm not giving up, ladies," she shouted over her shoulder. "I'll be in touch."

The ring that had formed around Betsy and the three officials dispersed, and a line of somber women filed past the two police officers standing on either side of the path. Some reached out and touched the cops as they went by, squeezed their shoulders to reassure them that there would be no challenge to their authority on this day, that everyone would do as they were told in deference to their shared history, their kinship ties, their understanding that we all faced an impossible situation. There was solidarity, even stability, in that impossibility.

But I had no such ties and I had no responsibilities. For me alone there were possibilities and I stood in that field longest. Even as Laura was pulling me away, I stood in open defiance and wondered what I'd do next.

One cop decided I wasn't worth whatever it would take to get me to stand down, and he headed back to his car with a shrug. But the other squared off and smiled. Slowly, he pulled his sunglasses off and showed me his close, ferret eyes.

There wasn't much to him, not enough to fear. He was all angles and knobs and weasely whiskers. So I smiled back. I knew what this boy was thinking: any man my age who was still alive and working on a farm alongside a bunch of women must be defective in some way, an easy mark. That's what made the rat show his teeth. That, and the fact that he had the gun. But he'd never given a thought to what necessity had done to men like me, survivors of a truly lost generation. Even the meekest us of knew how to fight off an assailant, how to strike first, how to crush the bridge of a nose with the heal of his hand. I brought up my fists and snarled like a pit-bull, or tried to. Suddenly, he looked uncertain.

A horn blew. The other cop stuck his head out the patrol car window and shouted, "Fitzy! Get your ass in the goddamn car! That faggot can't do shit!" Reluctantly, Fitzy backed away. Against his will, he returned to his own car, slid behind the steering wheel, and started the engine.

My heart was still racing as I watched them drive away. I cursed them under my breath, and I cursed myself for having nothing at hand but clumps of dirt to throw at them. Which I did, only to be showered in dust when the clumps hung and scattered in the first wind before the storm.

XII.

My hands were shaking. So were Laura's when she touched my shoulder.

"Just a stupid kid," I said. My throat was so tight I sounded half strangled.

"That's right," she said.

"Ah, hell," I said, blinking the dust from my eyes. "He's not the problem. He's just doing what he's told. They're the problem."

"Yes," she said.

"They never ask us to sacrifice anything" I said.

"You're right. They never ask. Let's get out of here before the rain comes."

"They never ask. They're always so afraid to admit that there's no simple fix, that we'll have to give up something to get something. They never ask. And then they take everything when we're not looking." Her eyes were red, but she wasn't pulling me away now. "It's our fault, I guess. We get what we deserve."

"Maybe."

I started walking toward the road. "It's our fault. But it's theirs too."

"So what are you gonna do about it?" Betsy had come out of the tool shed with a thermos of water in her hand. Purple clouds were tumbling over her head. "I'm curious," she said. "What are you gonna do?"

"What do you mean 'do'?"

"You sounded a little like your dad just then. Except that he was usually slurring and stupid by the time he got himself so worked up. I always wondered what he'd be like sober, if there'd be any action to follow his words. What would he actually do to them, given the chance to do something?"

"I wouldn't know."

"No, but you sound a little like I imagined he would."

"What are you getting at?"

"I'm gonna need all the help I can get if I'm gonna fight them."

"I wouldn't know where to start."

"I think you would." She scratched her chin and pulled the loose skin at her neck. "I think you're in exactly the right place at the right time. We'll be in touch."

Another blue flash shot through the clouds. Then the rain came hard and fast, and the dust turned to mud again. Betsy trotted back to the shed. Laura, her daughter, and I ran toward the road. Other stragglers shrieked and ducked for cover. There was a bass note of continuous thunder, a drum-roll of slamming car doors. A motorcade of shabby, workhorse vehicles filed into the street and joined a slow procession through old standing puddles and flashfloods of oily rainwater. Wipers failed to make any difference on windshields. Back-ends fishtailed at the narrowing curve behind the trees.

Laura fell behind. Her little girl was clinging to her leg. I stopped to wait for them as they stumbled along, all the slower for their headlong lunges, their feet slipping across the surface of the mud. When the lightning spit into the woods and cracked the earth, Laura shouted to me, "Get in the car. Don't even try to cross the street. Just get in and we'll go to my house until it blows over."

It was an old car like mine. A metallic green Chevrolet something-or-other with a grey interior. Inside, it smelled like lavender. The passenger seat was so far forward that my knees pressed up against the glove compartment, but I made no adjustments. The girl climbed in behind me; she was sniffling as she fixed her buckle, coughed once with a force that cracked the air. It was a dagger cough. Laura dropped into the seat beside me and leaned her forehead against the steering wheel. Her clothes were heavy with rain. Her pants were muddy to her hips. Her hair was dark and sticking to her face. A drop ran down her nose, hung from the tip like a jewel, and fell into her lap.

"When I tell you to get moving, you get moving," she hissed. The last thing the little girl needed was an audience to her scolding, so I was trying to mind my own business, watching the lightning arc and branch through the steam, when I noticed that Laura was looking at me.

"That's right," she said. "You. You can't just stand around in an open field at a time like this. With a big target on your back. Next time, I'm leaving you there. No way we're gonna get zapped because you're not smart enough to run when I tell you to run."

"Sorry," I mumbled.

"You better be," she said. Then she and the girl laughed. All three of us laughed as the rain knocked louder on the roof. "Okay, let's get out of here."

She turned the key three times until the engine rolled over and roused itself. Before she shifted from park, she looked at herself in the rear view mirror, brushed the hair from her eyes.

"We'll get something to eat, if I have anything," she said. "I know I have tea. At least we'll have tea."

A small, porcelain angel hung from the mirror—the kind of thing one hangs in memorium. Laura set it rocking with her index finger, a quick jab to the angelic face.

"We'll go home, dry off, and drink tea. Maybe I have crackers."

I couldn't do it. No matter how much I wanted to—and the closer I got to her, the more I wanted to—I couldn't let her take me home. The angel forbade it. So did the girl in the back seat, the bulge of her knees along her skinny legs, the cascade of her curls now straightened with the weight of the rain, the smudge of her nose, the way she shivered like a kitten. I could imagine a home for this girl more easily than I could remember my own: fairy wings and magic wands in a small, stuffy, sweet-smelling bedroom; in a corner, a row of dolls with unimaginably long legs and silver-yellow hair, shoulder-to-shoulder, a little old now in doll years but each grinning with equal radiance; on a shelf, a framed picture of the four of them cuddling together on their living room couch: Laura looking radiant in a plain white shirt; a straw-haired boy with handsome eyes holding a stuffed bear; a baby girl in footy pajamas with red fuzz atop her head; and him, square-jawed, clean-shaven, at peace.

"That's nice of you," I said. "But, you know, I shouldn't. It's already too late. I have work to do. And I bet I can outrun the lightning from here."

Laura's eyes narrowed.

"I don't want to impose," I said.

"You can't impose."

I wanted to wipe the rain from her face, to hold her wet face in my hands. "Of course I can," I said. "Perhaps another time."

She closed her eyes and nodded. "I know where you live," she said.

I opened the door, leapt out. "See you later, funny face," I said but the girl was no longer smiling.

I slogged through a gutter stream and scrambled up the mossy brick steps to Nate's house, slipping twice and scraping the heels of my hands on sharp edges. The thunder was so loud it seemed to stretch the sky; the booms bunched together until they created a single, continuous roar. The house was wreathed in blue light.

As I reached the top of the hill, a bolt landed close enough to blind me. Briefly, I stumbled in darkness. When my vision cleared, I was standing in the middle of Nate's driveway and my car was gone. There was nothing beneath the dead tree now but a shimmering mirror rising from the saturated muck.

I'd purchased that car for pennies when I returned from the front. I gave an old man what amounted to a week's worth of groceries for the right to take it off his hands. He was a sad case with wet eyes and a confusion deeper than senility. No matter how many times I told him I hadn't been wounded, that I hadn't even seen any action, he wouldn't believe me. He'd just put up his hand and say, "I cannot ask you for money." His Adam's apple would plunge in his stringy neck, he'd wipe his eyes with his sleeve, and he'd say "Put it away, son. You've given enough." Finally, I convinced him to accept a small fee, which was more money than he'd seen in months, and I drove away feeling like a con man and a thief. Thereafter, the car sat curbside for weeks at time, rusting at a leisurely pace when the pigeon-droppings and rainstorms weren't scorching the paint. Every morning I'd walk past it and think about the old man who wasn't sure where to find his heroes anymore. And I'd try to remember why I'd wanted his car in the first place, what errands I thought I'd be running. What roads would be passable. What visits would be worth the price of fuel.

Now someone had driven it away from me. The rain lashed my shoulders and pricked my scalp, the mud slurped into my socks, and I stood there in the open, mouth agape, completely exposed to a wrathful sky. Only a shot of thunder startled me out of my daydream. I looked again at the spot where my car had been, just to make sure that the disappearance wasn't a trick of light and shadow. Then I bolted too.

XIII.

"Ives," he said, pointing around his head. "The Fourth Symphony."

We were sitting at the kitchen table again and I was wrapped in a trio of towels as rough as sandpaper. I couldn't discern anything about the music.

"My car's gone," I said.

He slouched forward on his elbows as if we were finally getting down to business. "They took it?"

"Someone did."

"Foreseeable," he said, nodding. "Foreseeable. You must realize that we are surrounded by thieves and every species of vagabond."

"Nate, I have to ask you."

"William, I had nothing to do with it."

"I wasn't going to accuse you."

"Yes you were. But I didn't make the car disappear, even if I think it's the best thing that could have happened to you."

"Or to you."

"Perhaps."

In our separate ways, we studied each other for a long time. I cracked my knuckles and cleared my throat. The smell of rotten fruit, pervasive since the deluge, had worked its way inside now, under window tracks, over thresholds. An inescapable green air was upon us, which may help to explain why we were beginning to grow wary of each other. It was as if there was only enough air for one of us to breathe.

"They're shutting us down," I said finally, speaking only to forget my discomfort, scraped and bruised after slipping, my shirt still heavy on my back and drawing the heat from my skin, lightheaded from my near-submersion in the downpour.

"I was waiting for you to get to the point. I knew that something else was coming. I could feel the tension in the room."

"Three men from the town showed up with a couple of cops and sent us all home. They're going to take over."

"Increase the yield."

"That's what they say."

"Elizabeth must be losing her mind."

"I think she's seen this coming for a while, so it's more like she's arming for battle."

"Ah. And which Bastille are we going to storm?"

"I don't think anyone knows just yet."

He sat back in his chair at the head of the kitchen table and stared at the cornice, focusing on something I couldn't see. "The town wouldn't have moved on her without support from on-high."

"It's acting on state policy. That much we know."

"And the state's scared of its own shadow. It wouldn't have moved without the feds, not without federal backing."

"That's my assumption too."

"So it's national policy now, to reassert control over whatever arable land remains."

"My sense is that they don't appreciate people like Betsy running things, and that's about as far as they've thought.'

"Shortsighted."

"Certainly. Always. What are you getting at?"

"This is a reason to believe, isn't it?" His face seemed just a little smoother now, a little less wrinkled, and his shoulders visibly relaxed. "You have something in your life now. That's good. I'm happy for you."

XIV.

Another leaden front had moved in while I was sitting with Nate, not quite fog and not quite smoke but something in between: a low cloud, damp and particulate. It pressed up against the windows of the house and cinched out the night. Cut off from everyone and everything, we sat together for hours more, this time downing a couple of bottles of cat-piss vinegar that had been spoiling for years in the back of a coat closet.

After a few glasses, he started telling me stories about Walter: tender stories about Walter at the top of the Eiffel Tower, standing with his back against the steel girders, shooting pictures over the heads of the other tourists at the railing, too afraid of heights to venture any closer to the edge; ribald stories about their summers together on Cape Cod in the years before the plague, before their friends began to wither and fall in an autumn that seemed never-ending; bitter stories about their struggles with misguided family members and disappointed parents who'd had other plans for their favorite sons. "So many people thought he was a jerk," Nate said at one point, as if he was testifying under oath, "and I was never able to convince them otherwise. But I knew what he really was. I always knew."

When it was my turn to talk, I came up empty. "Mine," I said, "has not been a colorful life. I've always been a step slow. Until now, I suppose. Maybe I'll have a real story to tell some day."

"Better hurry up," he said.

After draining both bottles down to the dregs (which were numerous and unspeakably foul to chew), we parted for the night. As I walked the back path, Nate stood in the doorway, his cardigan hanging limp and murky from his shoulders, his hair unmoved by the gentle breeze of sulfur and soot. He struggled to breathe until, with a grunt of disgust, he stepped back and closed the back door.

By the time I entered the cabin, my eyes, nose and throat were burning again; my cough was a dry, rattling affair foretelling real danger; and I was hurting in less distinct ways as well. A stack of greeting cards caught my eye. Absent-mindedly, I'd left them on the counter beside the sink in the kitchenette. On top of the pile was a purple envelope addressed to George Stark in Dunwood, New Jersey from B. Stark in Colby. Embossed silver lilies against a lavender background: *"With Our Deepest Sympathies."* And inside, scrawled in familiar, loopy, childish letters opposite a perfectly-scripted *"You're in our thoughts and prayers"*:

Dear Brother,

I don't have words. Our babies should never die before we do. And people are assholes. All of them. Barb tells me it was something in the water Something they all new about. I wish there was a way to make them pay for your loss but I don't suppose there is ever a way to make them pay enough. They say the Lord works in mysterious ways and that's probably true. But maybe hes a little bit of an asshole too. You call me now whenever you want to talk. I hope that's soon.

Love,
Billy

I read it only once. Then I replaced it on the top of the pile.

When I'd begun the search a few days earlier, I believed it would change me. And it had. But not in the way I thought it would. I thought I'd find someone to love—in "kids," plural, I thought I'd find a connection I'd missed. But now I felt nothing. Or perhaps it would be more accurate to say that I felt this loss much less than prior losses, and that this loss only served to draw the others forward. There was no way for me to mourn this child. I could be angry about the circumstances of its death, angry that a Stark was among the first to go, the first of so many who would succumb to the despoliation—but that anger was not unique either. In fact, it was old and abiding and if I felt it with any intensity now, it was only because the numbers were piling up on me and I was growing weary of them.

XV.

Unlike the first two times I saw them, when they sprung upon me in the confusion of new circumstances and new settings, I actually wanted them to appear this time, willed them to come. And they did. Like fireflies, they called each other from the darkness, one, then three, then a dozen or more crisscrossing Betsy's farm in patters only they understood. I pulled the elastic band over my head, fitted the mask around my nose and mouth and gave chase.

I felt a fit coming as soon as I opened the door. Tasting something like bleach in the air, I heaved and choked and spit mucous into my mask. My eyes filled with tears. My stomach burned and clutched. On my hands and knees behind an untended privet, I twitched and grunted like a beast in a corner, waiting for the revulsion to subside. But I refused to cough. One sound from me and the lights would go out, the men would scatter into the woods, and I'd lose this one and only chance to do something noble. I reminded myself that I'd sung Stephen Foster tunes in the gashouse during basic training; I could do this.

Yet I didn't need to. I could have coughed an aria and no one would have heard. A shrill, metallic screeching was already filling the space between me and my adversaries, and there was no room in the atmosphere for any other noise. It blared at such a high pitch, at such a frantic pace, and at such a tremendous volume that it took me a few seconds to process what I was hearing. I ran through several options: emergency sirens, low-flying fighters, the scream of incoming ballistics. Then I thought I was hallucinating, that there was no way for the things of this earth to make such a racket without human intervention. But finally I realized that I was only hearing the crickets, hundreds and hundreds of them, reveling in their freedom, mating with impunity, singing to a sky that no longer supported their predators. It was as if they had fallen with the dew, a plague upon us—as if we needed any more signs from the heavens.

I trotted through the tall grasses with my hands in front of my face. At the roadside, I crouched behind a low boulder and watched the motion of the flashlights. Now I counted six, maybe seven floating up and down the rows in overlapping patterns, synchronized and deliberate. Maybe eight—all the lights were alike and none were still for very long. From the window of my father's cabin, at the top of Nate's hill, they'd appeared to move in fits and starts. As I crept closer, I wasn't so sure. The swinging glare of the flashlights whited out everything, altered my perceptions of depth and distance. There were men in the field before me, but I couldn't tell how many or how far they were from me. I crossed the road.

Overhead, the stars were so bright and numerous that the darkness seemed like the exception. The crickets were deafening. My lips and nose were wet in my mask. My hands were numb with my fear and too weak to make proper fists. I crept into the mud by Betsy's lettuce beds, waiting to be seen and ambushed, waiting to go down swinging. And, sure enough, the flashlights went out.

They were closing in behind me. I turned to see them standing shoulder to shoulder, a motley array of broken shapes, some long and crooked, some squat and round, like the numbers on a baseball scoreboard. They had their backs to the moon so I could only see them dimly, their faces demonic, their postures menacing, but there was something sad and pathetic about them as well. I couldn't tell what was wrong, but something was definitely wrong.

All at once, several of them, perhaps all of them, shined their lights on my face. Blinded and afraid, I stumbled back a few steps and covered my eyes with my arms.

"Hands down."

The voice was low and harsh and cut through the crickets with an eerie clarity. I kept retreating, involuntarily now as the voice whispered again, "Halt." Even the crickets halted.

"Who are you?" I asked, peering into the lights, hoping to catch another glimpse.

"Who are *you*?"

They closed in. I spun around and started to run.

"Stop now."

"I'm nobody," I said. And then I said something I can't quite explain, except that it always seemed to mean more than I expected. I said, "I'm George's son."

A flash of blue lightning shot across my eyes before I felt the crunch of the metal on my head. I felt the ground on my face before I knew I'd fallen. But before I lost consciousness, I heard someone say "no wait" and someone else say "shit."

XVI.

The world was white when I woke up, but I knew I wasn't dead because my mouth was dry and my head felt like it was split in half. I surveyed myself from the bottom up, wriggling my toes, flexing my legs, tightening my stomach, clenching my fists, until I knew I was still in one piece and that my head was the only source of the howling pain that wired through every nerve. From somewhere beyond the light I could hear labored breathing and three or four different hacking coughs.

Someone drew closer. "What? How the hell should I know? Give me that." An arm appeared through the white and two fingers reached for my eyes. I tried to turn but something held my head firmly as the fingers pulled down my eyelids. "What am I lookin' for again? Yeah. They're different sizes. Shit. Who hit him? You asshole."

Another voice said, "Alright. Give him some room. Back up. And turn the fucking lights off. No reason to dick him around any more than we already have. He ain't going anywhere anyway."

White to black, and then a soothing gray. I closed my eyes and braced myself for a change of position, a turn right or left in search of some relief. But the hands grabbed me again and the first voice said, "Hey fella. No sleeping now. Ain't that right? He ain't supposed to fall asleep if he's got a concussion?"

"I think that's right."

"Hear that fella? You better stay awake a while. Open those fucked up eyes of yours."

My eyes were adjusting to the darkness but my vision was still blurry and the face I saw above me, staring down at me, was horrifying. A jack-o-lantern mouth, a pirate's leer, long greasy hair like icicles in the moonlight. I yelped and slid backward a half a foot before the pain flattened me again. Then I heard laughter.

"Give him some room, man. You're scaring the shit out of him."

"Can't say I blame him. You're one ugly fucker."

"You're gonna kill him with that face."

"Hey, buddy. Is it the way he looks, or the way he smells?"

It was both at first. And then it was just the smell: urine and feces and sweat penetrating layers of heavy clothing. And something else too, something not quite human. I choked a little behind my mask.

"Okay. That's enough. Let's sit him up. Somebody give him some water." Several hands held my shoulders, supported my head, propped me forward, lifted my mask and tipped a bottle to my lips. The water was lukewarm and burned my throat. "Fine. That's enough. Let's not drown him."

I swallowed hard and closed my eyes as they lay me down again. The earth was cool under my head as the damp seeped through my clothes, but the ground was surprisingly firm. The fields had been soggy from the rain, but there was no mud beneath me now. I was cold, but not soaked. And when I opened my eyes again I could see the stars swirling through a canopy of forked branches.

"Where am I?" I asked, my voice betraying my fear.

"Don't worry," said the lead voice. "You're not far from home. We carried you into the woods, for cover."

"Who needs cover?"

"We all do."

I propped myself on my elbows and tried to get a better look at him, or at anyone for that matter. Then I could see them again, about a dozen of them in various stages of disrepair: one without a leg, one without an arm, a few leaning to one side or another, one with a flattened face, a couple with faces bandaged in frayed gauze, two hunched over. They were missing teeth, eyes, in one case an ear. Each was wearing some remnant of battle fatigues—a jacket, pants, boots—but not one of them was wearing a mask and not one failed to hack and spit as they stood there watching me.

I knew them after all. They were the casualties of the war.

They were, to a man, younger than me. In some cases it was probably the difference of a year or two, in some cases only a few months, but I was the senior man in the woods that night and I knew it because I was the only one who was relatively intact. The others had aged poorly in the hellholes of the planet.

In classrooms and boot camps, I studied the bombs, the chemicals, the pathogens that tore people apart—soldiers and civilians alike—only to be sent home with my guns still loaded, my fatigues still clean. But before me was a band of men who did not share my great good fortune, whose parents delayed copulation just a little too long and who therefore faced an earlier draft, a less thorough basic training, and an order handed down from the very top of the chain that they were expected to throw themselves into the smoldering remains of their own civilization. These were men who had inhaled the gas, who had caught the pox, who had crawled too close to ground zero. I don't suppose any of them ever fought at close range, hand-to-hand, although they all looked like boxers ten years after retirement, raw and twitching. More likely, they'd been at the mercy of the skies, ordered to squeeze off a few rounds before something truly wicked fell from who knew what direction and decimated them. And fall something always did, with great fanfare, leaving them in pieces, to be reassembled by modern medicine. And here they were, almost as good as new, jigsaw men stitched together from their own parts and returned to a world that no longer had any use for them.

My headache was mellowing into a respectable vintage, blooming a full range of symptoms and an elaborate aftertaste of blood and metal, but I was thinking clearly enough now to know the trouble I faced. "Who's 'we'?" I asked.

A black man stepped forward and took a knee before me. His right eye was a mere slit in a massive swelling that began at the bridge of his nose and ended at his ear. But his left eye was a kindly saucer that caught the moonlight and gleamed his youth; it was an eye that hadn't seen thirty years yet and was still, despite the dark things it had seen, radiant. He leaned toward me and touched my head with his hand. "This was a mistake, sir." I brushed his hand away but his regret seemed genuine and he just kept talking. "All the good folks are supposed to stay inside after the lights go out, but there you were. You can understand if these assholes get a little jumpy when someone gets too close, especially at night. If you're out at night, you're either lookin' for trouble or else you're someone who doesn't know the rules."

"I guess I don't know the rules."

"And why would you? You're here on personal business, the most personal kind of business. It's a terrible thing, to lose a father, and you gotta make your peace. That's the number one thing. But you better be a little more careful while you're making it."

"How do you know my father?"

"Pickled," someone said, and there was laughter all around. Someone else said "Stewed," and someone said "Cockeyed," and someone actually said, "Good ole' George." Then the leader spoke again, his voice like the rasp of branches blown together by the wind.

"George was our mentor."

"George was mental."

"Shut the fuck up. This poor guy's in mourning and you assholes bust his head open with a flashlight and now you're making jokes about the deceased and I've had enough of your bullshit. Apologize to George's son right now and hold you're fucking tongue before I bust you open."

"Sorry George's son."

"Don't mention it."

"As I was saying, your father used to give us a hand."

"He helped your gang?"

There was laughter again, but it was less generous this time. "We're not a gang, sir. We're the last line of defense." The men responded with murmurs of assent and some of them squatted to the ground around me and waited for the leader to speak again, knowing that he would tell their story, wanting him to tell their story. I wondered how many times they'd heard it under similar circumstances, while closing in on some hapless fool who'd wandered too close to their territory, and I wasn't anxious to find out what they did next, when the story was over and the fool was still sitting there, surrounded.

Until now I'd forgotten about the crickets, didn't even hear them above the throbbing pound and the ringing in my ears, but now I heard them again, keening as the moon dropped lower toward the horizon. And I smelled the familiar, inhuman smell hanging over the men. The combination of sound and scent was too powerful, rushing over me all at once until I fell back to the ground in a spell of dizziness and nausea. The leader paused, as if he knew how I was feeling and was offering me a simple courtesy.

"You can see what we are. The goddamn walking wounded. Ain't a man here who isn't maimed in some way, mangled like everything else in this wasteland. And if he wasn't maimed in the war, he's been maimed since, in battles with the fucking bums and losers who always seem to be hiding in the shadows of a place like this—which is what we thought you were." He touched his swollen face and grimaced. "I'm not sure what's worse sometimes, enemies dug in miles apart and lobbing heavy shit at each other, or assholes hidden in the trees waiting to jump you the moment you let your guard down. I'm sick of the whole thing, quite frankly—the secrecy, the cover of darkness, living hand to mouth. We all are. Yet we're nothing if not duty-bound. Dedicated to the security of our people. And we'll be damned if we let anyone, friend or foe, endanger the people we love." He turned his head and studied me with his good eye. "You still don't understand. We came home to what you see around you." He cleared his throat and spit into the dirt. "We came home to nothing, but we weren't ready to give up and we certainly weren't ready to give in, not to the pant-loads who took over in our absence. Like the fuckers who are taking over this farm."

"You know about that?"

"Shit. You really don't get it, do you? This place is a battleground. Food is secondary around here. It's the ideas that count. It took a full century of fuck-all to kill this place as dead as you see it now. One hundred fucking years of…what's the word? Right. Hubris. Charlie likes that word. Anyway, it was bad when we went off to war, and you can bet it was a helluva lot worse when we returned. Miss Betsy, bless her heart, has been trying to turn the place around for as long as anyone can remember, but what chance does she have after all that's happened? The best she or any of us could have hoped for was to keep it out of the hands of the motherfuckers who ruined this world in the first place. And that's what we've been trying to do ever since. And now we've lost this war too."

He tried to clear his throat but succeeded only in lodging something thick and wet in his windpipe. On his hands and knees now, he worked the phlegm through a variety of coughs, a range pitches, trying to find just the right melody to dislodge it. Like a yawn, the cough then passed through the rest of the men—and even I started to wheeze a bit—before the irritation subsided and the group was quiet again.

"Fuck that hurts," he said. "Worse every time. I'd wear a mask like yours but it's too late for me, for all of us. It was too late the day we got home. But we're good soldiers and we found some places where people were still hanging on, still fighting. Goddamn hopeless causes, every one, but we enlisted in every effort. We joined work crews, construction teams, fund raisers, but not one of those things were central to the problems we now face. Not one was going to save us. So, finally, we just went back to the land. Back to root causes."

"Literally," someone shouted.

"That's right. Literally back to our roots. Betsy's trying to keep up spirits and prove something with this place, but she knows it can't actually be done. It's too far gone. So she agreed to let us come here at night and do what she couldn't bring herself to do in the light of day."

I sat up so quickly that the planet seemed to fall out of its orbit. With both hands in the dirt, I clawed myself steady. "Fertilizer," I said. "That's what I smell."

"There you go, George's son. Now you're thinking."

"Quiet guys. He looks like he's gonna hurl. Give the man a second. You okay? You sure? Well you're right, in any case. We come in at night and spread the strong stuff, whatever we can steal from the town. So that at harvest time Betsy can declare the place a miracle." A high breeze knocked the branches together like dry bones. "But some damage is irreversible."

"My father was your middleman. He let you know what Betsy needed. At night, when no one was watching."

"For a price."

"Let me guess."

"We never felt right about it, if you wanna know the truth, but he was a grown man."

"Couldn't you have killed him with something worth drinking? I never met the man, but I'd like to believe the plastic bottles were beneath him."

"Believe us," someone said, the laughter swelling slowly among his brothers. "The plastic never even touched his lips."

Even the leader was laughing now. "No offense, George's son, but he's not lying."

"None taken," I said, "and my name is Will."

He patted my arm. "Good to meet you Will Stark. Call me Houston."

I nodded, very slowly. "So you're trying to help."

"We were. But we're moving on to Plan B now, and we're lookin' forward to it. That's when we fill the place so full of goodness it chokes on its own vomit."

"Sabotage."

"Your word. Not mine."

"Can't let them win, can you?"

"Ain't nobody gonna win now, no matter what we do. We just don't wanna give'em any satisfaction is all. There are good soldiers all over this land now, burn-outs with just enough left in the tank to keep the fuckers from feeling too pleased with themselves. Keep'em from forgetting what they've done to all of us. And that's what we're gonna do when the time comes."

Here-here, the men said. Mm-hm. That's right. Fuck'em good.

"And if there's any fertilizer left over after we're done scorching the place, we figure we'll just make a few firecrackers with it and blow up some other shit for good measure."

"Like the fuckin' Fourth of July," chuckled a man from the edge of a shadow.

"Ain't no other word for that except sabotage," someone said.

"Keep'em honest to the very end," said another.

Here-here, the men said. Mm-hm. That's right. Fuck'em good.

"What we really need is for the whole world to lay fallow for a little while," Houston continued, his good eye dropping to his shoes, "but that ain't gonna happen. So we'll just do this instead."

Right, they said. Say it. Fuck the fuckers.

I could sit up now, but only against a foaming tide of nausea. Teetering from side to side until I found a posture I considered upright, I held the grass for support and kept my eyes on Houston's meaty, tenderized face as it darted across and then circled my line of vision. Through gritted teeth—literally gritted; a few had been chipped by the blow to my head—I spit out the words, "What can I do?"

"See there, boys?" Houston said. "That's noble. That's why you shouldn't go cracking every skull that presents itself. Once in a while, it's the skull of George's son Will who wants to help. Will, let's be honest. We're nearing the end of this operation. Maybe we could use a spotter, George-style, for a day more. Maybe two. But after that, we're on to the next thing. You want a try-out?"

I leaned over and vomited between my knees. "Or maybe I try you out."

"That's fine too. Whatever you say. We're just glad to have a friend. Ain't that right? You go ahead and let us know what Miss Betsy thinks. And you can tell Mr. Nate that we're still watching things for him as well. He won't have no trouble for a while longer."

"What do you mean 'watching'?"

"How else does a blind man in a big fancy house survive with all the freaks crawling around? We own the night, baby."

"Oh yeah? You own the night? So where's my car?"

"How are we supposed to know that? Your car was stolen in broad daylight."

XVII.

They left me on Nate's doorstep, knocking twice before fleeing into the trees. He found me on my hands and knees, groaning. Expending all of his strength in one, concentrated burst, he lifted me to my feet. "Mercy," he said, "Glenden's become a brutal place, like all the others. What have they done?"

Clinging to me with his frail, chicken bone arms, he guided me into the parlor. He handed me a cup of hot tea, but the taste soured in my mouth and I handed it back.

It was better for both of us that he couldn't see me. I'd been manhandled and must have looked every bit as mangled as I felt. I'm sure that from certain angles I looked a good deal worse than that. My shirt was bloodied and torn at the shoulder: someone had tugged a little too hard, or else I'd snagged a branch as they lugged me past the tree line. Bits of grass and twig hung from my clothes, fell from my sleeves and pants as if I were losing my stuffing. Wide patches of mud swathed the places where I'd kneeled, fallen, been dragged, lay in stupor. I soiled his home with every step, passed on a bit of my shame—I had been mugged, after all; no matter how nice they were after they clubbed me, they still clubbed me—and Nate wouldn't have liked that one bit. He wanted no farm manure on his hardwood floors, no blood on his rugs, not when he spent his days padding from room to room in holey socks. And certainly he allowed no shit on his wing chairs.

But he could smell me—and smell I did, he assured me, "like a swamp in August." Like manure and petroleum and horsehide. Like the quickening of life and a premature death.

He handed me a warm washcloth. I ran it across my face ever so gently. I was capable, I soon realized, of inflicting real pain upon myself. An enthusiastic scouring around the eyes could send me into a swoon; a sudden jog of my head could cause the entire machine to shut down. The pain knifed through when I nodded, turned, looked askance at something. Sound made me queasy. I lost the thread of my own thoughts.

"Goddamn," I gasped. "Goddamn. What is that?"

The beginning of another old television commercial. I saw smiling housewives gliding through a department store decorated in red ribbon and cotton. A chorus line of clerks prancing, high-stepping, and handing over boxes wrapped in colored cellophane and foil, tied up with oversized red bows, precariously stacked in pyramids for the carrying, as the housewives kicked their lean legs, clicked their festive red pumps, pinched Santa's cheek, shook their round bottoms as they picked up their shopping bags and danced their way out a revolving door, into a happy chaos of yellow taxis and mewling tomcats and gray anvils falling from the sky. The knocking of a woodblock set my teeth to chattering.

"That will kill me, Nate. If it doesn't kill me, I'll kill myself."

"Oh, heavens. I'd forgotten it was even playing."

I moaned and shut my eyes as he fumbled with the controls, turning it louder before he turned it down to a faint whisper. Behind my eyelids, I saw flashes and bolts of terrible light. "Oh, please Jesus," I whispered, "make it stop."

"Gerswhin again," Nate said, apologetically. "'An American in Paris.'"

It took me a minute to register the quiet. "That seems about right," I said. "Turn them both off and spare us all a bit of our sanity."

"You have a point."

"Of course I have a point. Neither mean a damn thing anymore."

I rested my head on the chair back, unable to open my eyes, and dozed momentarily, until Nate said something that sounded like, "Slow to adapt."

"That's right. Too goddamn slow. They're overrun by earthworms and cockroaches. No more America. No more Paris."

"You make sense," he said. "I suspect that you're talking nonsense, but I seem to understand you."

"Can you imagine caring anymore? About Christmas shopping, or chorus lines? The earthworms inherit the earth."

He dabbed my face with a cold washcloth. "So you've met Houston."

"Black guy. A Cyclops. With a voice like flypaper."

"Sandpaper?"

"Stickier. He's going to lead the revolution."

"What revolution?"

"There will be no revolution. But he's gonna lead it when it happens. Gonna blow the whole thing apart so that it can't happen again. Nice guy."

"You can drink water, right? Water's okay on a concussion?"

"I don't know."

He put the glass in my hand and helped me tip it back. The water burned my throat again but I drank greedily, half-believing it would anesthetize me, or flush out the toxins. It did neither.

"So what will he blow apart?"

"I don't know. Probably just the children."

"William. William wake up."

"Yes."

"Not yet, okay?"

"It doesn't matter when."

"Okay. What do they want you to do?"

"Drink myself to death."

"No they don't."

"No, but they may as well."

"You've stopped making sense."

"I know. I would if I could sleep."

"Soon. Soon. Tell me what they want you to do."

"It was right there all along. The water that kills the baby. The cancer that kills the mother." He draped a blanket across my chest, tucked me into the seat. "The father drinks it all in and he dies too. It was all there to be drunk. Drinked."

"Okay, Will. Okay. Take it easy."

"I know. I know. My head's mushy. But I'm gonna help them blow the thing apart."

"Easy now, William. Take it easy."

I could feel my heart slow, and then I couldn't feel my body at all. My eyelids, which had been showing me Technicolor lasers and rockets, went black. I dreamed twisted faces, sharp teeth, and a falling sensation that twitched me awake again. I sat up and scanned the room in a cold, sweaty panic.

Nate was gone but the music was still playing at such a low volume that he may not have heard it, distracted as he was by the challenge of my injuries and his own blind triage. I heard every instrument, however, every finger on every string and all the spittle splashing into every bell of every horn. There was a moment of calm, of suspension, and then the glide of a trombone.

Later, a lullaby. A beautiful, blues-inspired lullaby—sad and sweet.

XVIII.

It was late afternoon when I woke up sweating beneath several layers of musty woolen blanket, drooling down my chin, seemingly drowning in my own fluids. I had slipped a foot or so down the back of the wing chair while I slept so that my weight now rested uncomfortably on the base of my neck. My right hand had fallen from the arm of the chair, dangled a while, and was now full of needles and pins. Somewhere behind my eyes was the pain of fracture. I struggled forward, kicking the blankets across the room. Orange light flooded in from beneath the half-drawn window shade; the dust swarmed in a slanting drizzle to the floor. In one of the adjacent rooms, a beam popped and the house sighed. I coughed, swallowed, and waited for my strength to gather.

"Are you awake?" Nate asked. He was nestled in the corner of the couch, as still as the furniture, a very old man content to wait for me in the shadows.

"I suppose."

"I left a glass of water on the table beside you. Right there."

"Thank you. I needed that."

"You talked in your sleep. You said, 'What would your husband say?'"

"That doesn't sound like me."

"Perhaps not. But that's what you said. I've been sitting here all the while, keeping an eye on you, so to speak, worried almost as sick as you, and you're rude enough to tease me with innuendo."

"Don't know."

"That's a shame. I rather liked the idea that you were still dreaming about sex. No one seems to have the energy for sex anymore."

"Fine. I was dreaming about sex." We listened to my body for a while, monitored the flow of lymph and humours, waited to see what if anything would burst as I prepared to stand. "Did I say anything else I'll regret?"

"Not really. Just some ominous musings on water, death, and your willingness to take up arms against baby-killers. Other than that you seemed quite normal."

"How about you forget all of that," I said, standing now. "Just chalk it up to a bad night."

"It's already forgotten," he said, but as I left the room he added, "Please tell Houston to spare the innocent."

I continued down the hall, then paused with my hand on the doorknob and listened for a moment. The house was quiet. "Nate," I called.

Weakly, from a distance, "Yes?"

"Thank you. For what you've done for me."

I didn't wait for an answer. No answer would have mattered. Instead, I opened the door to a bright evening and stepped out.

Two black birds darted from the footpath. Their feathers were slick and smooth, iridescent around the crown, and their wings were fleet and sharp. In one motion they ascended and careened into the trees, two arrows cutting through the long light, and something in my chest leapt with them.

"Nate!" I shouted. "Nate, open some windows! It's okay! Open some windows!"

The air was so clear and cool, in fact, that my lungs burned with it when I inhaled. My eyes dazzled a little. And every ache and pain in my pummeled body flared at once before sputtering and guttering away like a blown candle. The scent of cut grass and rotting leaves gusted along gentle currents and sound seemed to travel great distances: I heard a truck grind into gear, a bird's song, a backfire or shotgun cracking, and, nearby, the rattle of metal tools in a wooden shed.

"Hope is a dangerous thing." Nate was behind me, just off my left shoulder, his soft face lifted to the sky.

I opened my throat and gulped it down, the whole mirage of hope and health. "I'll take it," I said.

"What do I hear?" he asked. There was a loud crash, followed by a bowling-pin tumble and a muffled but savage run of foul language. "Ah. The profane Miss Elizabeth. I thought you said she was gone."

"I thought she was."

I started out walking but ended up skipping down the slate path to the street. Less than a day earlier, I'd crept down this same path in a low crouch, stalking the shadows I took for crop thieves and vandals. Now, beneath a deep and cloudless blue turning gray, I surrendered to the hillside. The plates of my skull knocked together with every step but I ignored the pain and swung over the low stone wall at the roadside. Momentum carried me across the street, through the gravel lot, and toward the slapdash structures that stored the farm's only capital, where I came to a dizzy rest against the side of the tool shed. I could hear Betsy cursing inside when I knocked on the doorframe.

"You," she said. "What do you want?" She stacked one plywood crate on top of another and slid the stack across the dirt floor without looking up at me.

"Nothing. Thought you might need a hand."

"You keep showing up."

"So do you."

"I'm just collecting my things."

"Me too," I said.

She continued to work as she spoke, her red swollen hands in constant motion over leaf rakes and small trowels and earth-cutting blades and an ancient oilcan stained orange after several generations of hard labor. "Have you found what you've been looking for?" she asked.

"I guess. Yeah. In a way, I guess I have."

"You know, it's ironic but he was wiser than the rest of us," she said. "That's what used to piss me off. He wasn't trying to be wise, after all. He was just trying to be left alone. He didn't like to be exposed or set himself up for failure. But, in hindsight, it's pretty clear that there was a wisdom in his madness too. Only a wise man has as little regard for his betters as he has for himself."

"Or maybe a wise man knows he has no betters..."

"Yes, that too."

"…and therefore stops trying to prove anything."

"If that's the mark of a wise man," she said, "then George Stark was the wisest man I've ever met. He died just as the world was catching up to him."

She unraveled a bolt of netting, re-wound it tighter around a cardboard tube. "So you planning to stay for a while?" she asked.

"I don't know. Maybe. You?"

"Where would I go?"

"I don't know what I'll do if I stay."

"Yes you do. Same thing I'll be doing—living a little, fighting a little, trying to figure out what's next until there ain't nothing next."

"Hm."

I remained in the doorway, watching her work, as dusk fell. It grew so dark in the shed, with twilight at my back, that I could barely see her eyes now. But I could feel them when they focused on me, when she stopped moving, finally, and stood before me with her fists on her hips. "Do me a favor tonight, would you?"

"Sure. What?"

"Tell Houston it's time. Tell him to go ahead and salt the fields. And thank him for everything And tell him I love him for what he's already done for us."

"Are you sure you want me to do this?"

"Not at all. No. But you should do it anyway. Promise me you'll tell him."

"Okay," I said. "I promise."

XIX.

It was still there, taped to the wall over the bucket of trowels: three x's across the top, three running diagonal from top right to bottom left, the rest o's. A tick-tac-toe grid and, until now, a code to be cracked, a mystery for another day:

X   X   X

O   X   O

X   O   O

I'd been staring at it repeatedly since I arrived, often for minutes at a time, believing that at some point the meaning would leap out at me, as it ultimately did. If I'd found it among the scraps on the floor, or stuck between the cushions of the couch, or even folded and pressed and stored in a manila folder in the kitchen drawer along with his expired driver's license and a vaguely-worded military commendation, I'd have thrown it away and never given it another thought. But it was taped to the wall, and in the chaos of my father's cabin, that gave it pride of place. It was important and I wasn't about to take it down until I knew something about it.

And now I knew that it was a working map of Betsy's farm.

With the nub of a broken pencil, I added my own mark, corner to corner across the entire page:

X

John Tessitore has been a newspaper reporter, a magazine writer, and a biographer. He has taught British and American history and literature at colleges around Boston and has directed national policy studies on education, civil justice, and cultural policy. He serves as Co-Editor Across the Pond for The Wee Sparrow Poetry Press. His poems have appeared in the *The American Journal of Poetry, The Wallace Stevens Journal, The Ekphrastic Review, Gastropoda, Wild Roof* and elsewhere. He has also published four chapbooks available at www.johntessitore.com.

www.johntessitore.com
Twitter: @JohnTessitore2
Instagram: @jtessitorewriter
TikTok: @Jtessitorewriter

www.ingramcontent.com/pod-product-compliance
Lightning Source LLC
Chambersburg PA
CBHW071336140726
47996CB00005B/2000